The Secret Library

Essential sensual reading

The Thousand and One Nights

3 sensual novellas

The Thousand and One Nights
Kitti Bernetti

Out of Focus
Primula Bond

The Highest Bidder
Sommer Marsden

The Thousand and One Nights – Kitti Bernetti

When Breeze Monaghan gets caught red-handed by her millionaire boss she knows she's in trouble. Big time. Because Breeze needs to keep her job more than anything else in the world. Sebastian Dark is used to getting exactly what he wants and now he has a hold over Breeze, he makes her an offer she can't refuse. Like Scheherazade in The 1001 Nights Seb demands that Breeze entertain him to save her skin. Can she employ all her ingenuity and sensuality in order to satisfy him and stop her world crashing about her? Or, like the ruthless businessman he is, will Seb go back on the deal?

Out of Focus – Primula Bond

Eloise Stokes's first professional photography assignment seems to be a straightforward family portrait. But the rich, colourful Epsom family – father Cedric, step-mother Mimi, twin sons Rick and Jake, and sister Honey – are intrigued by her understated talent and she is soon sucked into their wild world. As the initial portrait sitting becomes an extended photo diary of the family over an intense, hot weekend, Eloise gradually blossoms until she is equally happy in front of the lens.

The Highest Bidder – Sommer Marsden

Recent widow Casey Briggs is all about her upcoming charity bachelor auction. She doesn't have time for dating. Her heart isn't strong enough yet. But when one of their bachelors is arrested and she finds herself a hunky guy short, she employs her best friend Annie to find her a new guy pronto.

Enter Nick Murphy – handsome, kind, and not very hard to look at, thank you very much. And he quickly makes her feel things she hasn't felt in a while. A very long while. Casey's not sure if she's ready for it – the whole moving on thing. But as she prepares to auction Nick off, she's discovering that her first hunch was correct – he's damn near priceless.

Published by Xcite Books Ltd – 2012
ISBN 9781908262080

Cover design by Madamadari

Contents

www.xcitebooks.com

Scan the QR code to join our mailing list

The Thousand and One Nights
by Kitti Bernetti

Chapter One

SEBASTIAN DARK'S HAND CLOSED over his rival's and gripped it in a crushing hold. 'So that's a deal then.' He smiled like a cheetah leaning over a gazelle – in for the kill. A sheen of sweat broke out on the smaller man's upper lip; the smell of defeat punctured the air. Seb regarded his rival distastefully.

They had battled.

Seb had won. He always won.

Smaller companies swam into his business waters at their peril. Shark-like, he gobbled them up and swallowed them. This takeover meeting at one time would have excited Seb enough to produce an erection under his smart Savile Row trousers. Now he had made a bigger fortune than he could spend in a hundred lifetimes. And he had to admit as he looked past his vanquished foe and surveyed London through the floor to ceiling windows of his plush boardroom, *he was bored.*

'Thank you for your time Mr ....' what the hell was happening to him? He had just bought this man's ailing company for a cut price five million and Seb couldn't even remember his name.

'Vanhoffer,' Seb's assistant Richard Waters, hissed in an aside.

'Mr Vanhoffer. It's been nice doing business with you.

I'll show you out.'

The man stood paralysed at the door of the wood panelled boardroom. Seb towered above him. Placing a hand on the little man's back to guide him out he noted the man was trembling. With anger, with remorse at losing a company that had taken him a lifetime to build and an hour to lose? Seb barely cared, that was business. Protocol required him to be magnanimous to the foe he had just destroyed. He escorted Mr Vanhoffer down the cream carpeted passage to the lift on the 21st floor. He stifled a yawn as the lift doors closed.

Then, a vision caught his eye so startlingly perfect, so eye-catchingly tantalising he, along with the other men moving about their business, faltered as if in slow motion and stared. It had happened again. The one thing that had sparked Sebastian Dark's interest in months was igniting the city suite of offices like a sky-rocket on bonfire night. She was wearing black patent stilettos, business-like, up to a point. But with a cutesy bow that made him want to grasp those spiky heels and slide them off, to trace his fingers over the stocking mesh covering her oh-so-pale skin, to stroke toes that would be painted in-your-face kick-arse red.

He wondered if she realised that as she walked, she placed one foot directly in front of the other giving her a Marilyn-Monroe sway that teased and more than suggested the up and down thrust of a good hard fuck. Yup, he conceded, she realised it all right. And she used it. To give her power. And control.

Richard broke the silence. 'Goddammit, that girl is sex on legs. Just wait till that perfect arse goes by. The things I wouldn't do given one night alone with her ...' All thoughts of the vanquished Mr Vanhoffer had disappeared once the blonde beauty sauntered into view. 'They call her the Ice Queen, gorgeous but untouchable.' Suddenly remembering himself and looking sheepish at Seb's granite stare, Richard tried to stop gawping. But the girl's magnetism drew both men in. The tight black pencil skirt moulded over buttocks as round as a young pony's, the breasts fettered behind a virginal white shirt and oh so artfully pushed up by the files she was gripping. Her ample mounds bounced against the top button as if they longed to be released. And finally those go-to-bed lips, strawberry red glistened at them like a half-bitten cherry.

Apart from himself, Seb noted, enthralled, she was the most controlled human being he had ever encountered. Why was she like that? What was it that made her turn away from everyone, eschew office parties, push people away? The Ice Queen. Fascinating. Controlled and as arctic as a steel ice-pick. She knew every guy in that passageway was hooked. And every woman was puce with envy. It was as though she was playing a game. She was a winner, like himself.

Only Sebastian Dark was determined there was one game she wasn't going to win. Because he was going to stop her. Tonight. After dark. He'd been plotting it for weeks. Ever since he had discovered that she was the one who'd been sneaking in after hours and had the bare faced cheek, the high handed effrontery to have been embezzling thousands from his company – milking it, skilfully, for months. From under his very nose. And she thought he didn't know.

She had reached him now, so close her perfume itched his nostrils. She glanced at him under thick eyelashes, tossing her blonde fringe in that insolent way until she caught his stare and momentarily she stumbled. One foot went wrong on the thick white carpet. For a nanosecond her step was less than sure. As he raised an eyebrow, she disappeared into her office. Closing the door with a sharp rap. The fascinated glances of those in the passageway dissolved. As soon as she'd gone the electricity charge disappeared and people flowed back into the business of the day.

Tonight Sebastian Dark would catch her. In the act. Tonight he would punish her. The only question was how?

He would enjoy that. Enjoyment? He'd almost forgotten what the word meant. All he'd ever wanted was business success, his adrenalin fed on the next big deal. Now he had it all – a fortune, women who threw themselves at him. But enjoyment eluded him. He felt crushingly empty. Until now. Something stirred beneath his tailored suit, the sleeping length in his groin twitched and hardened. She fascinated every man who saw her. And ignored every one. He smiled; he wasn't going to be ignored by the Ice Queen. Suddenly blood rushed through his veins and spiked his cock to attention. It felt good. He was alive again.

Breeze Monaghan dropped the files she was holding. They spilt across the floor like a fan. She clung to the wall. If its solidity hadn't held her up, her shaking legs would have crumpled to the floor. She couldn't go on much longer.

He knew.

Seb Dark was a smooth operator; somehow he had found her out.

But he couldn't possibly know. She had been ultra careful. Besides, he was too high up the pecking order to be in the least bit interested in her, an interim accountant, a faceless paper pusher. Still he terrified her. Looking down his nose at everyone like an eagle spotting prey. Dangerously masculine. *Pull yourself together* she practically shouted then clamped her hand over her mouth. The strain of living a lie for months was beginning to tell. She had to quit, like she had in all the other places. But not yet. She just needed tonight to complete her plan. She breathed deep, pulled herself upright, grabbed the files and thrust them into order.

No one must find her in this state. She knew they called her the Ice Queen behind her back. That was the only way she could protect herself and she did it now. Putting back her mask of control. Cooling down her fear of being found out. Just another few thousand was all she needed. She sank

4

at her desk and smoothed down her dyed blonde hair. She longed to go back to soft chestnut, be natural. Living a lie was starting to eat her soul. She pulled the desk drawer open, slipped her manicured hand to the back and pulled forward the little photo in its oval frame.

They were the ones she was doing it for. Her mother – soft focussed but with an inner core of steel, just like Breeze. And Breeze's sister, Summer, sweet as a country meadow, her wide eyes so vulnerable. Her frail body so crooked.

Everything Breeze did she did for them. She would milk the last few thousand from Sebastian Dark's monolith of a company. Then she'd disappear just like she'd done so many times before … Only she had to get tonight over first, and then escape, before her boss with his cruel eyes *really* suspected something.

Chapter Two

'HEY, MISS MONAGHAN.' THE security guard's face lit up as if he'd been waiting for her. 'Comin' back to the office to work late again? You put in far too much time for this company, you know. You should be out enjoying yourself instead of hunchin' yourself over that desk until the early hours.'

'You still haven't told anyone I come back at night have you, Ronald? If they thought I couldn't complete my work in an ordinary day, they'd think I was incompetent. It's our little secret, isn't it?'

'No way, Miss M, I haven't told a soul.'

She'd loved Ronald's cheery smile. If only she could say goodbye properly but then that would give the game away. Thieves, like beggars, couldn't be choosers.

The lift doors swished open. The offices were best when they were like this: empty; still; safe. Her heels were silent on the plush carpet. She was perfectly in control. Until she passed the spot where Seb Dark had stood today and regarded her with that inscrutable stare. She shuddered. You never did know what that man was thinking. If he wasn't such a threat, she might have found that sharp taunting jaw intriguing, the wavy sun-kissed hair attractive, the broad shoulders worth fantasising over. She slapped the idea down; she had work to do, work that demanded all her powers of concentration.

Breeze sat down at her desk and flicked the computer into life. It had taken her ages to hack into the protected full accounting system. After that it had been a painstaking

6

matter to find all the dormant accounts and start programming them to divert their funds to the suspense account she had set up. Bit by bit over the months her plan had been executed. Finance companies like this which dealt daily in millions always had hidden cash that had slipped through the net. A clever accountant like her had only to look for those little pockets of wealth and grab them. The secret was not to be too greedy. To take what had been forgotten and make it yours. Tonight she would siphon off the money she had ring-fenced, direct it to her secret offshore account and close down all evidence of her wrongdoing. She was pleased with her plan; it was a thing of genius. Virtually undetectable.

It took her two hours to garner every last penny, to check and double check that all her tracks had been covered. And finally to insert a worm into the accounting system that would eat all the evidence of her crime from the firm's hard disk, hiding her treachery as surely as if she had turned back time and it had never happened. Her shoulders were sore, her back stiff from tensing up. Then, she heard the opening of a door down the passage. Who the hell was that? She hadn't heard footsteps, no one else had ever been here at this time, it was the middle of the night. Whoever had opened that door must have been there all along. Bile rose in her throat fit to make her vomit. In an instant she had shut down the computer, grabbed her bag and shot up from her desk when suddenly the handle on her office door clicked and turned. Like a gunshot it tore through the night's silence.

Sebastian Dark filled the doorway, shutting out the light with six foot four of six-packed male. His voice as menacing as a fisted hand struck her like a blow to the chest. 'It seems you suffer from a great deal of insomnia, Ms Monaghan.'

'I ...' thoughts flailed about in her head as she struggled for composure. 'I had to finish the quarterly report. It's all done now, I was just going.' She shot him one of her devastating smiles and watched it land on stony ground.

'I don't think so, Ms Monaghan.' He raised one eyebrow and squared up to her. She tried to breathe but it felt as though all oxygen had been sucked from the room. There was no escape. She glared at him.

'Let me out. I want to go.'

'You're going nowhere. Unless you want to go to jail, that is.'

'I don't know what you mean.' She spat the words out, like a cornered rattlesnake ready to strike. Attack she'd always found to be the best form of defence. It had certainly worked when she was a child defending her sister from the bullies who taunted her. Breeze stared insolently back, every bit the Ice Queen. She'd get herself out of this, she had to. Her mother and sister depended on her. They were the only thing that mattered in this whole crappy world.

'You know exactly what I mean.' He slid into the room and slammed the door firmly behind him. 'You're a bright woman. And gorgeous into the bargain, that's a great smokescreen, making people focus on your looks to distract them from what you're really up to underneath all that makeup and tight clothing. You're as clever as the finest of my executives even though you've hidden your genius well. The thing is, I always wondered what you were doing with all that intelligence. Always suspected that you had a hidden agenda. I've been watching you. And now I've caught you.'

He was bluffing. He had no idea what she'd been doing; what's more she'd fixed everything now. He was five minutes too late. She puffed out her chest; she walked to the front of the desk. She wasn't scared of him despite the cruel spark in his gaze. He was only of interest as a tool to get her what she needed. Funds to support the only two people she had ever loved and who depended on her. All the same, her hands left uneasy sweat marks on the desk. 'You can't prove anything.' She felt her throat constrict as at five foot two inches she craned her neck to look into sharp grey eyes flecked with silver shards which stared into her very soul.

'Maybe, maybe not.' He left the words on the air; he was toying with her, like a cat with a mouse.

'If you don't move aside and let me out, I'll scream blue murder.'

'Really.' The side of his mouth quirked; was he finding this amusing? Certainly he was enjoying the sport. In that second, she despised him.

'I'll scream rape. I'll tear my clothing, bloody my face and rub it over your beautifully laundered white shirt. Let me aside.'

She moved to push past him when he grabbed her arm. His eyes betrayed a mixture of contempt but what was the other light shining there? Desire? She'd never seen that in him before. Had even felt a tiny crumb of respect that he was the only man in the building who hadn't ogled the blonde bombshell look she'd worked so hard to project. She'd thought he was a robot, a money- making-machine, devoid of interest in the opposite sex and yet here was more than a flicker of lust. Here was a smouldering volcano. And she wanted none of it. His stare traced the curve of her breasts, lingered on her hotly glowing skin. Brazenly he raised his hand and slid it down the front of her shirt. His fingers were hard, his palm cool as he moulded it around her breast. Like a traitor, her heart went into overdrive, thumping so heavily that anger, and she had to admit, a spark of attraction, shot back in his direction.

'You can scream as loud as you want.' He edged closer, his words small puffs of breath teasing her ear. She could smell his scent, lemon, leather, power. 'And not only do I know what you've been doing but I've had a camera hidden and trained on your monitor for weeks. I have every movement you made on that computer screen on film. It's all the evidence I'll ever need. So it wouldn't have mattered, Ms Monaghan, whether you'd wiped every damned computer in my whole business because I've caught you.' He began to massage her breast, registering with satisfaction the agitated rise and fall of her ample chest. 'Red handed. Like a rat in a trap. You're mine, whether you like it or not.' She wanted to strike him, would happily have killed him. How dare he defile her like that, how dare he take what wasn't his, how dare he fondle and stroke until her stomach started to swim and her crotch began to moisten. She opened her mouth to swear at him then caught that heated desire in his eyes again. Lust, need, hunger. For a woman who was holding a losing hand, that might just be her trump card. He wanted something. If not, why hadn't he just called the police?

Then, releasing her, he moved aside from the doorway. 'Feel free to go if you want.'

She nearly took flight. Then realised he had only offered it because he knew it wasn't an option.

'But I'll catch you.'

Bastard.

'What the hell do you want?'

He sauntered over to the leather chair opposite, sat down and placed his feet in their handmade shoes on her desk. His legs seemed to go on forever. 'To be entertained.'

She narrowed her eyes at him. 'You're mad.' Rich, powerful successful men all had an element of the psychopath in them.

'Possibly you're right,' he sneered. 'I really should just have you marched off the premises. You've been stealing from me for months. But I find you an enigma. I'm interested in you. Not much, don't get your foolish female hopes up that I'm keen in any way, or that I'm falling for you, although I have no doubt many men do. You do interest me though.' He nodded his head slowly and she was mesmerised. His voice was a low rumble. He didn't need to raise it; he had enough command merely in his presence to keep any listener enthralled even if they did hate his guts and want him dead.

'And I need to be entertained. You see I've grown bored

of all my other pursuits. My bank balance is overflowing. What's more, at the end of this month I turn 30. That milestone has been troubling me because all I've ever done is work to make money, 24 hours a day every day of my 29 years. By sheer sweat and bloody mindedness I've achieved every goal I've ever wanted. I can have any woman I choose but what I need is another challenge. And you're going to provide it. You're going to make love to me and you're going to make it the most thorough, the most extraordinary sexual experience any woman has ever given a man. So much so that I'm going to want to come back for more. You're going to do it weekly for a month, at least until I turn 30. You're my birthday present to myself. Perhaps then, and only then, I will decide you have paid off your debt.'

'But I ...' Her words settled on silence. She couldn't. Wouldn't whore for him.

He put his hand up. 'I'm not interested in hearing no. I'm a good judge of character, Ms Monaghan. One thing I have worked out is that you aren't like other women. You're too distant, too self contained. For some reason you hide too much of yourself and although I think I could wine and dine any woman in this building into my bed, I know I couldn't buy you. But by trying to con me out of my money, you've handed yourself to me on a plate. This business card has my personal phone number on it. Think up something pretty damned amazing, Ms Monaghan. Or perhaps now we know each other a little better I can call you Breeze. Phone me tomorrow without fail. Tell me where and when you're going to entertain me. And just remember, I have eaten in all the best restaurants, stayed in world class hotels. I don't need that any more. I need something different to excite me. And it had better be good, or I'll make sure your whole damned life comes crashing around those cute, sexy feet of yours.' He got up, ignoring her stunned expression at his outrageous proposal and flicked his business card at her as if he was tossing pennies to a beggar. 'You must have heard of

Scheherazade and the 1001 nights. You're going to be my own private Scheherazade. You've played a dangerous game against one of the biggest players on the scene and now it's payback time. Goodnight.'

Chapter Three

BREEZE ROLLED SHEER BLACK stockings over buffed thighs and clipped them into emerald green suspenders. A green silk triangle hid the dark bush at the top of her legs betraying her natural hair colour. She eased oversized breasts perfumed with Chanel into a bra which barely contained them. It was an absurdly expensive set of underwear but instantly the feel of it, the soft silk, the tightness of the suspenders started to bring out her sensuality, made her move like a languid cat. Sebastian Dark meant business.

She'd heard enough stories of his ruthlessness to know he demanded a flawless performance from everybody he worked with and she had to give it. Because she knew if she didn't Seb Dark would slap her into jail and throw away the key. That would leave her mother and sister alone and there was no way she would fail them, they'd been failed by too many other things in life. She was their only chink of sunshine in a cruel world. If this was what she had to do, she must do it.

She pulled a clinging jersey tube-skirt over her ample rump, and topped the simple outfit off with a tight ribbed jumper which hugged her like skin-tight leather. As she did so she thought about her phone conversation with Seb this morning. 'So where are you taking me?' He sounded languid, still in bed. At the thought of his slender hips and what lay nestling between his thighs, Breeze tensed.

'To the sea. To Brighton.'

To her surprise, he laughed. She'd never heard him laugh before. 'The seaside. Well, at least it's different. I haven't been there since I was a boy.' His voice over the phone was gravelly, darkly sensuous.

'We'll catch a train, I've reserved tickets. I'll meet you in the carriage at Victoria station.' Her voice was brisk, no nonsense. She knew he was about to protest, suggest they take his car and chauffeur but no, she was going to make the big billionaire rough it, besides she had plans for that train ride. Briskly, she'd told him a reserved seat number and before he'd had a chance to protest had rung off. He'd be there. She smiled, she'd hooked him.

As she walked down the platform in her high boots, heads turned. She may have been dealt a rough hand in life, a selfish, feckless father but on the looks front she had scored, big time. She wasn't showing any flesh, and a warm chunky jacket covered her top, but her bottom in its tight skirt mesmerised men like they'd been hypnotised. She spotted Sebastian alone in the six-person carriage. There was only one minute before the train left and she'd deliberately turned up late. She wanted him on edge; she wanted him playing by her agenda. No one else would be using this carriage; she'd reserved all six tickets.

His eyes were hooded as she noted him sit up to attention at her approach. As she opened the door and stretched her leg to take the steep step she saw him jerk at the cheeky glimpse of white skin above her stocking tops. 'You're cutting it fine, aren't you?' He was clearly on edge, just what she wanted.

'I made it on time.'

The train moved off into the evening sunset shining on the Thames and they were alone, delightfully, securely alone for the half hour journey. It wasn't long, but it would be enough to get Seb nicely warmed up. This was the hors d'oeuvres, Brighton was the main course. The train began to pick up speed. As she removed her jacket, she smiled inwardly to see his eyes widen at the way her body was displayed, a perfect hourglass under the skinny jumper. He

14

shifted in his seat. She smoothed her hands down over her bottom, liking the feel of her hands against her body. He'd forced her into this but somehow she was enjoying calling the shots. The prospect of holding an incredibly good-looking man in her thrall, perhaps the most powerful man in the city wasn't entirely unpleasant, especially one whose gaze was as intent as a panther's.

Breeze peered at him under long lashes. 'You must be hot in that coat, why don't you take it off?'

He did as she bid, and tossed it aside. The early evening lights of London suburbs twinkled on as the train chuntered and sputtered over the tracks. 'Sit back down.' Again he did as she asked, the air in the carriage crackled with tension and the scent of his aftershave, spicy, woody, entirely masculine. She liked his suit, crisp cut, beautifully tailored. 'You don't mind if I take this off do you?' She pouted and grasped the jumper, wriggling her way out of it, making full use of the action to shake her luxuriant hair over bouncing, fettered breasts, forced up in the silky bra to display a magnificent cleavage. 'And this skirt is way too tight for comfort.' The corner of her mouth uplifted as she saw Seb involuntarily lick his lips. As if he was hungry, starving in fact and at that point she wondered how long it had been since he had been truly sexually aroused. He'd said she'd interested him and by implication that the women who threw themselves at him, bored him.

Had he perhaps in his ruthless way been tracking her for weeks, months even as she'd made her way around his offices? Had he plotted being this close while biding his time? Had he fantasised a moment like this while sitting all alone in his penthouse apartment? Had he enjoyed the hunt, purposefully delaying the gratification for his own amusement and was he now coming in for the kill? The thought excited her, sent a throb of expectation to that secret place at the top of her shapely legs.

She stood before him and pulled up her skirt till it

15

tightened sluttishly over her rump, displaying the green silk knickers, the sheer stocking tops, the tightly clasped suspender belt. Then she turned around and at that point the train jolted throwing her forward so that she lay sprawled across the seat opposite Seb giving him a grandstand view of the cheeks of her rump spliced by the tiny green panties, thrust upwards towards him. The train had stopped opposite a row of back to back houses, the carriage close enough for people to see in. As Breeze turned her face to glance at Seb, she was shocked to see they were being observed. A man at one of the windows, in the act of drawing his curtains had halted, fascinated to see Breeze, arse-upwards, with Seb, now on the edge of his seat intent on her display. Her legs, like the sides of a triangle, still in long boots were too much of an invitation for Seb. He kneeled forward, holding back no longer and ran his hands up over the leather boots, slowly, lingering over her thighs and then, glancing himself at the man watching, he moved aside the green silk panties.

Breeze had never been spied on before. Her reaction surprised her, startled her. Suddenly she felt excitement pool in her belly at having a voyeur witness Seb's expert caress as he started to probe with his fingers over her pinkly swelling sex. What previous sexual encounters she'd had in her lifetime had been tame. She had always held herself aloof, never letting men get close though many had tried. And now that she had been forced by Seb to take on the role of sexual temptress he was threatening to stir and kindle something deeply buried within her psyche. Like a cat curling to wakefulness, opening its green eyes wide and flexing its claws, she felt a reckless sensuality glimmer within her. Who would have imagined someone as controlled as her would put on a show for a complete stranger, would have unfolded herself, exposed her female charms in public for men she hardly knew? But she was in control, just where she liked to be.

Breeze was fully pumped up now, could scent her own

16

musky moistness as Seb stirred and whisked at her soft swollen sex. Involuntarily, she heard herself moan. 'Slowly, please,' she begged. 'Moisten your fingers, make me wet all over, play with me.' Was that really her giving Sebastian Dark, the richest, most powerful man she had ever encountered, orders? And yet, he was fired up by her assertiveness. Besides, she had nothing to lose. He'd told her to make it good and that had given her a freedom to uncover the hidden depths of her own sexuality. She wriggled her arse higher, jumping as his fingers slipped deeper into her peachy wetness. His breath was warm on her buttocks. His touch was delightful, probing, long, satisfying. He dipped his digit into her depths, using her own juices as lube, helping her to delicious wetness. As she glanced back, she saw him look challengingly at the spectator who stared in amazement, pressing his face closer to the window, to get a better look.

As they both watched the man, frustrated, trapped behind the glass, Breeze felt Seb fondle her buttocks in one cool hand, pulling her upwards. Then, she yelped as she felt his tongue come down over her exposed crack, warm, slippery, eager, hungry. He started to lap her up hungrily, to lick at her, to tongue her sweet pinkness. The sensation was glorious. No man had ever approached her brazenly from behind in such startling intimacy. The smuttiness of it fired her to arch her back, spread her knees and buck against him, to work herself up and down on the fingers pounding inside her.

The man at the window had opened it now, was leaning out desperate to steal a better look. And as he did so, Breeze saw him unzip his trousers and pull out his cock. Just as he frantically started to pull at it, the train jumped into life and rolled away. A low chuckle emanated from her throat to think of the voyeur missing the best bit, missing the climax because she could feel, she knew, very shortly, that Seb was going to bring her to that magical place. To a place she had never been before. To a place she had only read of and now was about to experience. And his touch was so expert, so controlled, she knew any second now as his fingers worked faster, ever faster he would bring her there. She clutched on to the rough wool of the seats, felt the train rock back and forth, felt its vibration churning up through her knees through her thighs and straight to the soft swimmy core of her cunny. Glorious, extraordinary sensations sent waves of ecstasy over and over again where Seb's tongue licked and probed and pointed mercilessly. As he worked at her, taking her up, up, making her sweat, she heard him grunt, 'Are you ready? Are you ready for me to make you come?' Oh God, was she ever? She was readier now than she had ever been, nothing and no one had made her want like this, made her need like this till she thought she would burst if he didn't bring her to fulfilment.

'Yes, yes' she screamed the words, over the pounding train noise, couldn't help herself. He rose instantly from his knees, still with his back to her he grabbed her around her straining breasts and pushed his fingers down the front of her sopping wet panties. There, immediately, he found the almost painfully swollen bud which was crying out to be stimulated. Like a jeweller, polishing a precious diamond, he placed the soft pad of his thumb against her aching clit, whilst thrusting a strong erect digit deep into her sex and moved each in glorious, mind blowing unison. Breeze could barely stand it any longer, her tits tender and raw in his grasp, he MUST bring her off, she would die if he didn't. 'More,' her voice croaked, then louder, 'more, more please. Harder, much harder.' And he did. So gorgeously he did, rubbed, moulding and rolling, pushing and whisking around her clit, deep into her tight little opening until finally in one totally and utterly mind blowing push and thrust, she felt the orgasm explode like an earthquake through her entire body. Starting at the tip of her clit it came, he kept working her until she came again and again, and again shuddering, pounding like the train's wheels thundering on the tracks. Would he ever release her? No, he was enjoying being the master too much, forcing her to climax over and over, juddering her body against him, moulding her into the hard, stiff erection that pushed into her back until finally, exhausted and crumbling, she collapsed onto the seat in front of him. He exhaled, his short breaths telling her that he had achieved his objective, he had brought her to the precipice and taken her over it. He had won but so had she. She felt sated, waves of exhilaration drifted over her body. Her first orgasm, the first time she had been aroused enough, the first time a man had taken such a commanding lead with her and brought her there. She lay dreamily, as if she were floating on a cloud.

He sat next to her; he placed her head in his lap. He stroked her forehead. She nestled small there. Then in a show of tenderness she found surprising, he placed butterfly kisses on her forehead. Soft and light he helped her come down from ecstasy into sheer, restful delight. He wasn't to know it was her first orgasm. She wouldn't tell him. But possibly he sensed something amazing had happened to the woman lying before him. They weren't friends, they weren't lovers in the proper sense but perhaps under that razor sharp exterior, there was somewhere hidden inside him a human being who sensed another's extraordinary moment.

Chapter Four

THE TRAIN BEGAN TO slow; the last of the evening seagulls swooped and cried in the sky announcing their arrival. Brighton station was coming into view. Breeze regained her control, stood herself up and covered herself but couldn't help seeing Seb's erection tight against his trousers, magnificent and unspent. Although she resented his hold over her she knew she was as excited as him as to what the evening would bring. He had stayed in control, had allowed his cock to harden but not to climax, but she was determined as they stepped out of the train that she was going to be in control of the rest of the evening.

'So where are we going now?' he asked.

As they walked down Pavilion Parade, it felt odd. It felt as if they should be holding hands like all the other couples jostling towards the sea front. They'd shared intimacy and yet this was still just a business arrangement.

'To the pier, it's where everybody goes.'

'I've never been to Brighton before.'

She turned wide green eyes on him as they made their way around the Pavilion with its extravagant turks cap roofs lit up for night time. 'You've never been to Brighton? I would have thought every Londoner had been here.'

'Not me. I've only ever devoted my life to making money. Ever since I was a teenager I don't think I've ever done anything or been anywhere without that one express purpose. Fun hasn't been top of the agenda, and that's what people come here for, isn't it?'

'Absolutely, the whole place is a pleasure dome,

shopping, swimming, cavorting, eating.'

'Sex.'

'Yes.' Her nipples hardened when she saw the expectation shining in his eyes. She even blushed to think of what they had just shared, on a train, with a spectator. 'It's the original dirty weekend location.'

'So, you're going to take me to the Grand Hotel, are you?'

'No way, big-shot, that would be too boringly predictable. Tonight, you're roughing it. Besides I've got something much more thrilling in mind.'

As if driven by her words, he grasped her hand, enclosing it like a bear's paw holding a mouse's. Normally cool, she found it was warm in the night time air as he steered her carefully between the traffic, across Marine Parade and onto the wooden boards of the pier. He was stunningly good looking, she thought, as girls gawped with their friends watching him striding by, his dark coat blowing behind him in the wind. But intimidating. People stepped aside for him. It suddenly struck Breeze to wonder why on earth he was doing this. With his wealth he could have had countless women, gone to all the exotic places on earth she could only dream about. And yet he'd chosen her, a straightforward working girl who didn't even like him. She guessed it was a billionaire's privilege to be contrary. They walked down past the tacky jewellery booths, past the ghost train and the helter skelter. At the end of the pier, they stood in front of the garish lights of The Crazy Mouse, listening to couples' screams on the Galaxia. The sweet sickliness of pink candy floss tinged the air and the sound of frying doughnuts at the stalls echoed the excesses of a place solely designed for indulgence. 'That's where I'm taking you.' Breeze pointed upwards and there, on the edge of the pier, soaring high above the sea was the Air Diver Super Booster. 'That thing scares the hell out of me.' As her chin craned upwards to watch the massive crane-like structure rise slowly upwards, even Breeze felt queasy. She was conscious of Seb gripping her hand harder as they watched the capsule with its wary looking inhabitants climb ever skywards, piercing the night sky. A small coterie of expectant watchers had gathered in silence, their mouths open. When like a stone dropping, the capsule shot downwards, the people inside screeched at the top of their voices, the watchers underneath ducking as it shot past like a giant pendulum, rising in the opposite direction to drop again and scare people nearly to death once more. 'I've always loved this place; it's wild and crazy, a place to escape to.'

'That's where you're going to entertain me, is it?' Seb looked intrigued, a spark of adventure, the uncharacteristic sense of pleasure for pleasure's sake gave his expression a new animation.

'That's it,' Breeze pulled him over to the ride's entrance. 'You said I had to make it good and believe me this ride is going to be the best. Not scared are you?' she taunted.

He threw his head back in amusement emitting a throaty laugh more energised than she would have credited for a money-making-machine like Seb Dark. So, he *could* have fun if he really tried.

The fairground man said, 'Take your shoes off both of you and leave them on these shelves. The Booster's 130 feet tall and you'll be going up 38 metres above the crowd. We don't want anything dropping on passers by from that height. He strapped Seb and Breeze in securely opposite each other. Two other seats stayed empty, no one else daring to ride this one. 'There you are, safe and sound. Enjoy the ride.' He winked. It was like being in a straightjacket. Seb looked at Breeze, his composure steely as they moved up, suspended in the air. 'It gives me butterflies going up this high,' Breeze said but Seb's look was entirely challenging, waiting for her to make her move. The tension mounted with every foot they climbed. She wanted to catch him just at the right moment, get him exactly as the fear and the

22

exhilaration were about to begin. She looked at him straight on.

Seb thought he'd never seen eyes that green. In the half light they were like a sultry feline's, always challenging, always gutsy. But behind them and behind the "look at me" blonde hair was a subtle, captivating beauty he couldn't take his eyes off. Seeing her, tasting her on the train had ignited him so that he'd almost dragged her here. What the hell she was going to do this perilously high in the air he had no idea until she started to wriggle and squirm and slide downwards in her seat. She just managed to prop her feet up to settle on his knees. A little more wriggling and she managed to get her stockinged feet into his lap. 'Undo your zip,' she invited.

He swore feet were one of a woman's most underrated erotic instruments. Breeze's enticed him. They were, like the rest of her, beautiful. Dainty, long, athletic-looking, sheathed smuttily in the sheer black stockings. As she positioned herself, he glimpsed the tantalising sight up her skirt of the delights he had tasted earlier, her neat chestnut bush hiding her strawberry pinkness. It had been a surprise but now he realised the blonde hair was just part of the facade she had built up. Who was the real Breeze? That was the challenge.

They rose ever higher, the pier below now nothing more than a thin strip, the people clusters of pinheads. His excitement began to mount. He eagerly dragged the zip downwards and freed his cock from its boxers. She had nearly brought him to fruition earlier with her rear display, as brazen as a whore, as classy as a duchess but he had held back. He was a master of delayed gratification; well used to slow, deliberate business deals. Holding back always gave him a greater thrill in the end.

He was already erect, had never really softened from her escapades on the train. His cock ached now with tension as she placed her stockinged feet around it. The bulbous head peeked out as she expertly gripped and started pulling and pushing, so, so gently, her knees splayed apart, her green triangled silkiness displayed for his delectation. Her smooth white thighs glowing in the moonlight. The funfair ride had momentarily peaked in mid-air, had reached its zenith prior to tumbling. They were held there in the night sky, increasing the excitement, ratcheting up the expectation. Seb's cock was afire now, brimful and ready to shoot as Breeze massaged it firmly. He gripped the sides of the ride, his knuckles whitening. But still he held back, and still Breeze worked at his jerking cock. The pressure was almost too much to bear, his balls tweaked, her feet went up and down, the stockings stroking his shaft, the tip emitting a bead of precome.

She knew exactly how to work him, how to cause his blood to pump, how to splay her wares so that his eyes couldn't leave her beautiful crack. Her feet encased him, squeezed the top of his cock, rode over the sensitive head, driving him wild, so that he almost grabbed himself and finished the job. And yet he knew what she was doing, she was waiting, her timing perfect knowing that the sensations would be intensified once they were flung downwards. That would be her cue to rub fast, so fast she would bring him to … And then it happened. They were plummeting, descending through the air; his heart leaped into his mouth, a rush of adrenalin like a snort of cocaine zoomed to his prick, made him yell out loud. And at exactly that point Breeze wanked his shaft, faster, faster, faster with an expert pressure that made him climax so violently, so deliciously that a spray of creamy come shot out so far and so fast he thought he would never finish, projecting as they pitched through the night air, away, across the sea, far away into the crashing waves below. The sexual release was like ejecting a cannon, like shooting an arrow. Leaving him panting, gasping for air, a thundering roaring in his ears. Expertly, as the fairground ride pendulum-like swung upwards then down again, she eased the pressure but carefully finished him off, a smile spreading across her face, as satisfied as the cat who's lapped the last of the cream.

She was incredible, mind-blowing, better than any drug. She'd sucked everything out of him. He gasped and laughed like a baby. Something about the terror of the ride, combined with her ice coolness had taken him to heights he'd never imagined. At that point, watching her grin of satisfaction, knowing that she had got as much out of giving pleasure as he had of receiving it, he knew he wanted to possess her. Had to know the sensation of being inside her. Totally claiming her. When, when would that come? It would be the ultimate. He had to have it.

They both staggered off the fairground ride, amused that the people around them suspected the speed and the height had made them unsteady on their feet, whereas they knew they shared their own dirty little secret.

'Dinner now, I am starving.' Seb pronounced. He chose Brighton's best restaurant, drank its most expensive bottle of champagne. He wanted to keep her, didn't want to let her go, wanted to spend the entire night with her, see her naked, feel her warm under his fingers, know all of her. They approached the steps of the Grand Hotel facing the front, the one that had the most desirable views over the beach. They would wake up late, make love and breakfast like kings. 'Let's choose the best suite, the penthouse, they're bound to have one.'

'I can't.' She turned away.

'You can't?' He was wrong footed and that was an experience he didn't often have. No woman had ever refused him.

'No. Not tonight.' Her green orbs were impenetrable. He was too proud to ask when, when would she sleep with him properly? 'I ... I'll see you next week. Next Saturday. Like we planned. That was the deal, wasn't it?'

Despite himself, he felt bereft, let down, deflated. This had felt like the start of something. And yet here she was turning away from him. Yes, that was the deal but ... 'Why do you have to go? It's so late? We could share the same suite.' He looked down; this wasn't a role he had ever played. 'We wouldn't have to share the same bed.' He turned his eyes to meet hers again. Need ached somewhere within him. But not just a sexual need. Was that the sound of him almost begging? Would this be the one time in his life he had hankered for something and hadn't won? The words had formed in his head and come out without him planning them. And yet they were real. For once, he found himself being sincere. The man who never gave himself away, the man who never let anyone see his true colours was here in this lonely seaside town asking for her company.

'I can't.' She smiled. It was a genuine smile, simple, open, it was at odds with the aggressive blonde. 'I ... I have things back home I have to attend to. I'll phone you Saturday. As agreed.'

'No wait,' he stood in front of her as she turned to go. 'Then we'll drive back, I'll hail a taxi to take us to London.'

'No way,' she held up her hand, 'that'll cost a fortune.'

He laughed hollowly. 'A fortune? I've got one of those. Don't refuse me, Breeze.' She was silent and the resentment he had seen when he'd first accused her of stealing, closed over her face like a mask. They were strangers again, and as strangers they rode back to London with her sleeping curled away next to him on the back seat, a woman who he desperately wanted to reach out and touch, but who might have been sitting a million miles away she was further from him than ever.

Chapter Five

BREEZE TRIED TO OPEN the front door silently. The big old town house creaked at the best of times, and most of all now that she didn't want to be discovered. A light shone down the passageway from the cosy kitchen. She was pleased when she entered it that it wasn't her mother but her sister, Summer, who had waited up for her.

'Is everything OK?' Summer's speech was slurred as always, sounding as if she was drunk. When in truth it was the cerebral palsy that had been with her since birth that hampered her body although her mind was as quick as a fox. She was so brave though, she kept the house clean and bright for Breeze and their mother. There were fresh flowers in a vase and the smell of bread she had baked that afternoon wafted through the kitchen. Summer had made this her kingdom, her bit of the world where she wasn't judged or laughed at for not being normal.

'It's fine thanks.' Breeze wore a different mask here at home. But it was still a mask. She had never told her mother and sister how she afforded to keep them in the faded grandeur of their Edwardian house. They just thought she had a fantastically well paid job and worked hard. They weren't to know that the repairs had long ago stripped her wages and that she'd had to scheme and commit wrongdoing to preserve their sanctuary. The house had been built by Breeze and Summer's great grandfather. Their father, who had gambled, had nearly lost it all before he left their mother for a young girl. Breeze had worked hard at her studies to become a professional woman, all so she could preserve her family's home. Keep the one thing that ensured they were safe and secure, that bound them together. Every time she came through the door she thanked heaven they were still here.

Sebastian Dark threatened all that but at least tonight she had not only managed to hook him, but to keep him. He hadn't phoned the Police. Yet. She was still where she belonged. She kissed Summer goodnight and made her way upstairs. On her bed lay open the dictionary she had taken from their small library to study the story of the Arabian nights and Scheherazade. The humble vizier's daughter who risked death every night at the hand of the king unless she told him a story to save her life. Each night though Scheherazade stopped in the middle of the story in order to keep the king coming back for more and so save her own life.

As Breeze fell into bed, with thoughts of what it might be like to spend a night with Seb Dark she knew she must be wary of letting that happen and most of all must never give herself entirely to him. For then, he would discover that she was a virgin, that the Ice Queen had never fully given herself to any of her lovers. Surely, once he had gained that prize, he would discard her and lose interest and she would then end up in some jail and this house, their sanctuary would be lost, her family broken up.

Breeze turned on her side and tossed the book angrily to the floor. She must never let Seb or any man get close. Her mother had been right when she'd thrown her father's photo in the bin forever, "Stand on your own two feet, Breeze. Be independent; make your own way in life, live like an island and you'll never be disappointed."

Seb clunked the door of the high performance aerobatic aeroplane shut and fastened the safety harness over his chest. He often flew when he had a problem. It helped him to focus, brought him back to his business. In business he was a one hundred per cent success. In his private life he wasn't so sure. He pulled the plane upwards, over the bright sunshine-lit city sky and looped into a turn. It was Saturday; it had taken an age to come. He'd never known a week to go this slow. He'd leapt out of his skin when Breeze phoned this morning. For seven long days he'd wanted to speak to her, see how she was. But he had been too proud. No woman was going to bring him to his knees. Besides, theirs was a business arrangement, wasn't it?

He snaked the nippy aeroplane along the Thames which sparkled like a stainless steel ribbon. The gherkin building stood proud and quirky, the Shard reaching up sharply into the London skyline like a dagger was nearly finished. His business had helped finance all of the landmark buildings he loved. He'd helped to build this city and yet how much of it had he really seen? Only places where he'd had meetings. And even when he'd been invited to sports events or the opera there'd always been the corporate boxes where he could chat sotto voce and do business. Business – the be all and end all. Breeze had told him in her phone call to meet her outside the Albert Hall this evening and he'd felt oddly elated. He'd been there with a business client but had remembered nothing apart from the deal he'd struck, had ignored the music.

Were his life's memories destined to be nothing but a series of deals? At the end of this month he would be 30 and would face something momentous, a benchmark in life. He'd had the first third of his life. Had he fought and battled for the right things? He looked at the tiny matchstick figures of people rushing over London Bridge. What drove those men? Wives, children? Aspirations that Seb had always seen as a weakness, ties he had actively avoided. And yet for other men that was what life was all about. Suddenly he felt cavernously empty. Then, a freak gust of wind careered across his wings, buffeting the plane, sending it off its axis. He yanked the controls, struggling, fighting to keep it in

29

check, another buffet pushed him to the left, the plane careered madly, frighteningly. For a second he thought he'd lose it, his chest constricted, his hands gripped the controls so tightly his fingernails dug into his flesh until finally, he righted it. Turned it quickly and headed back down the Thames towards the airfield and safety. It had been close; he'd lost concentration, something he rarely did. He'd been thinking of Breeze. His whole life could have ended then and there. As he stepped out of the plane and towards the clubhouse and his chauffeur he wondered who would mourn him if he had lost control and plummeted. Breeze. Would she care? She would probably be pleased – after all, it would free her. He smiled wryly to himself, she'd probably even come to his funeral. Knowing her, she'd be dressed in red.

She'd told him it was a gala performance tonight, with black tie and evening dresses. As he stepped out of his car, he saw her instantly, head and shoulders more beautiful than any of the other women flitting like butterflies, trying to be noticed.

He stood for a moment as he got out of the car. 'Is something wrong, sir?' George, his chauffeur enquired.

Seb realised he had been staring, drinking Breeze in. 'No, no, you can go now, thank you. Collect us at 11.' She stood out like an ethereal moth among the other garish women. She wore palest lilac silk, a sheath so simple, it draped around the curves of her figure like petals unfurling around a blossom. The back of the dress dripped downwards leaving her shoulder blades, and the curve of her waist exposed and the moment he saw it he wanted to stroke his fingers down the track of her spine. As he made to walk over, another man approached her with an open smile and immediately, Seb wanted to push him to the ground. He walked faster. 'Breeze …' He took possession and steered her away. 'You look absolutely ….' Fabulous, gorgeous, beautiful? No word he could find summed her up, 'Perfect,' he settled on. It would do.

'Thank you.' Her eyes, sea green, lingered on his tall figure, the hand-stitched suit with its satin lapels, the neat black bow tie. 'You're looking pretty good yourself. The perfect English gentleman.'

'With perfect manners?' His mouth twisted, his clear eyes alert to the irony in her voice.

'I hope not,' she challenged. As he steered her through the crowd, passing each door of the imposing round red brick building, he felt wisps of the few curls that had escaped her tumbling up-do and floated along the line of her bare back. Her hair was softer today, more natural; he stroked it down-like underneath his fingers.

People stared at the stunning couple as she led him up the red carpeted stairs, past the glowing chandeliers. Hundreds of people filled the building. 'I trust we're going to get some privacy here somewhere.'

'Don't worry.' She turned back and he saw colour creep into her cheeks like the first tinges of bronze on autumn leaves. 'I have a very good friend who works here. She manages all the props; she's staged something very special for us. You won't be disappointed.' When they reached the floor where the stairs ran out, the crowd finally thinned to nothing. There was a sign proclaiming, "Gallery, CLOSED for this performance". She looked around quickly to make sure they weren't being observed and pushed the door. He had only ever seen the Albert Hall from a private box where he had been in the centre of the crowd, right down there with the performers. Up here felt different, hidden. The cool stone floors empty, the black ironwork stark, the crowd buzzing with expectancy way below as they took their seats for the performance, not a single one of them were aware of the two people sneaking into the top floor, high above them. There, in the middle of the deserted balcony, stood a four poster bed. Like something out of the Palace of Versailles, its base and elaborately carved head was glistening with gold leaf. The blood red curtains around the bed were tied back with sumptuous gold chord, the velvet counterpane pulled back to reveal white Egyptian cotton sheets. A pleasure dome, especially and secretly placed.

Seb felt his mouth go dry. Surely she wasn't brazen enough to want him to take her here; it would almost feel like a public performance with all those snooty, concert-goers in their penguin suits concentrating on the highbrow classical performance below. Breeze beckoned him over. He stood before her. The entire auditorium which had been buzzing had now gone quiet, the orchestra was about to start. A clamour of applause arose as the conductor took to the podium. Breeze's curves were a work of art, her shoulder and back like the rounded body of a violin. The subdued light shone on her, making her skin as smooth as a swan's breast. Seb swallowed, the hairs on the back of his neck bristling with expectancy. This was his chance to possess the woman who had been tormenting his thoughts, the woman he had to admit who had plagued his waking hours and many of his dreams for months. As the first echoing strings of the violins started their melody his blood stirred.

Seb wanted to unwrap her slowly, like the best present at Christmas time. He reached out and ran his fingers up her hand. She flexed it at his touch and he denoted a shiver of pleasure run through her. Her skin glowed, he could scent exotic bath oil, cinnamon, cloves, lilies and he realised she must have spent the entire day getting ready for him. Imagining her preparations, soap running down her body, her hands creaming the soft skin of her breasts began to fire his loins. As he stared and stroked, the peaks of her breasts hardened under the silk of her dress. He stood closer and leaned in, breathing her as if he were drawing in the essence of a bottle of the finest chateau d'yquem wine. He placed his lips on her collarbone and kissed along its line. Her skin was divine. Seeing her nipples in sharp relief under the sheer material made his cock spring to attention. He wanted her to desire him as much as he desired her. A pulse at her neck ticked, first slowly, then faster as he ran his kisses up her neck, over the sultry mounds of her breasts. She tilted sideways and as she did so, the heart-searing notes of the violins and cellos below echoed the mounting beat of her heart, shuddering against her dress.

Then, as if they were executing a complex mating dance, she made a move, gave him the contact he yearned for. She brought her hands up behind his neck and pulled him to her. He leaned down, and brought his lips on to her open mouth. She tasted of all things sweet; honeyed fruit, sun-ripened syrup. Her tongue sought him out, played with his. Her body pressed against him, she hesitated a second on feeling the gathering erection bulging at his fitted trousers, then moulded herself into it as their kiss deepened. His fingers skittered over her back, he felt the tremors of desire vibrate through her and he could bear it no longer. He had to see her, drink her in fully. Seb gently peeled her away, held her in front of him, watched the sheaf of her dress rise and fall as she panted. Then, edging the straps of her dress down her shoulders, he let it fall and crumple to the floor. She was wearing not a stitch apart from a little gold chain and an amulet at her neck, her naked body glowed in the half light and he knew he wanted to consume her. Every tiny morsel of her.

He knelt in front of her and buried his face in her thighs, felt them tighten with expectation. The music rose through the floor, vibrating through her. She placed her hands on his neck and pushed his face into her bush. Soft, delicate, scented, he needed to taste her. He couldn't wait any longer. He stood, picked her up in his arms and flung her on the bed, watching her full breasts jiggle tantalisingly to rest. In an instant, he had spread her legs, was kneeling at her entrance and staring at her splayed like a decadent white and pink orchid before his eyes. He took his fingers and parted her, then in a second was tasting her, had his lips against her throbbing clit and was swirling it with his tongue. He played her like the finest musicians were playing their instruments, bringing his hand up cupping her warm eager breast, watching her stretch and curl in response. His fingers grazed over her nipple, raising its peak to hardness, feeling her shudder with ecstasy.

He needed to be inside her. As the music grew louder, its power firing his rock hard cock he needed the bliss of her closing around him. He raised himself, threw his jacket to the floor, began to undo his belt but then, as the music changed, softening and mellowing to a lull, Breeze took over. She sat up and pushed him to lie down before her. She knelt, almost demure, and released the clips in her hair to let it fall over her pendulous breasts. He gasped at their heaviness – they were like rich ripe fruits hanging from the tree ready to be plucked and he reached to fondle their fullness. She ran her hands up his shirt, undid each button with trembling fingers, unfolding the rich cotton to reveal a muscular chest. Then she moistened her lips with her tongue, leant down and placed them full over his nipple.

He was surprised at this move; no woman had treated his nipples to this delight. Then, as she straddled him with her buttocks trapping his throbbing member, she started to wriggle on him while she suckled his nipples with her mouth. She jiggled and bucked her sex against him squeezing and riding his erection, driving him wild. He realised as she slid her cunny up and over his cock moistening it with her juices, covering it in her musky scent, rubbing its length along her swollen clit that she was in danger of bringing herself off. He squeezed her tits harder, hearing her squeak at the little jolts of pain as he gripped her nipples, her fleshy globes full and heavy in his hands. He could bear it no longer. He wanted to win the prize of bringing her to orgasm while he was inside her. Grabbing one of her glorious bouncing buttocks in his hand, he raised and stilled her while he grasped his throbbing cock in the other.

Its shaft was glistening with her moisture, its length solid from the pressure of feeling her buttocks and clitty ride over it. He found her gash and thrust himself inside her, her squeal of ecstasy drowned in a crescendo of violins as Seb grasped her tits again. His fingers were wet from her beautiful juices and her eyes flickered shut as she rode him like he was a bucking bronco and she was a rodeo rider. His expert massaging of her moist tits pushed her into overdrive, her buttocks slammed against his thighs, her slickness drove up and down over his cock, her tight passageway sucking and pulling at him as he delighted in her superb wetness lubing him. Oh God, he could stand it no more, her voluptuous body shaped like a guitar was the perfect instrument for driving him wild, he opened his mouth and cried out as he felt the spunk forced up inside him shoot into her as she pumped mercilessly, opening her eyes and connecting with him, looking into his soul as she drove him, rode him forced him, to mind-blowing orgasm just as the drums thumped, the cymbals crashed, the might of the whole orchestra filling the Albert Hall drowned out his yells of orgasmic fulfilment.

He felt sleepy, exhausted, fulfilled. If the world ended in that second he would be a deliriously happy man. The bed was superb, gilded, over the top. The beautiful Albert Hall, rich and red, was extravagant, echoing the way he was beginning to feel about Breeze lying next to him. Ice Queen, she was not. He turned towards her supine beside him and noticed goose bumps. 'You're cold.' He gently covered her over, pressed the warmth of his body close to hers. A sudden rush of protectiveness engulfed him as he swept his hand around her and hugged her close. He didn't want her to be cold, didn't want her to be hungry or unhappy. These were new alien sensations to Seb.

In his offices, she had been icy. When he had caught her stealing from him she had been fiery, everything about her said, "keep away". But after he had possessed her, she was like some secret garden fenced off with iron railings which once the gate had been unlocked was soft and fragrant, dewy and feminine. The music floated upwards to them, they lay as if in their own secret tent. The rest of the world, the hundreds of people below didn't matter. It felt to Seb as if he had waited a lifetime to feel this close to another human being and now he had a glimpse of what the rest of the world meant when they said that money couldn't buy you happiness. They meant moments like this. The warmth, the closeness, the intimacy. He reached to the gold chain at her neck, a heart encasing a tiny diamond. 'This is pretty, a gift from a lover?' A pang hit him somewhere deep in his chest. Jealousy! Something he had never experienced before. It hurt.

'No,' she looked on it fondly, 'From my sister, for my 18th birthday. She saved for a year to buy that. I wear it all the time; it's my most treasured possession.'

Seb let the light shine on it. 'You're lucky to have a sibling you care for. I had a brother, once. An elder brother.'

'You *had* a brother, what do you mean?'

'He was ten years older, and the complete opposite to me. He was artistic, a photographer. He went to all the exotic parts of the globe, shot the most amazing things; I still have a portfolio of his work. My father idolised him, the first born son and all that. He died in an accident in South America photographing in the jungle. My father never got over it. I suppose that's one of the reasons I devote myself to business. I wanted to prove to my father I could be a success too. I don't have an artistic bone in my body; my only talent has been in building businesses. It's ironic though because my father has no respect for business, he thinks we're all crooks, that we do nothing to enrich the world.'

'That's sad.' She turned moss green eyes on him that shone with compassion. 'You're so successful. Your father should be proud of you.'

36

'I wish someone would tell him that.' Suddenly, Seb felt exposed, raw. And he wondered why he had shared that with her. He would never normally betray such weakness to anyone. What was happening to him? It made him feel slightly uneasy. Then he remembered their lovemaking and realised that she had still kept something from him. Perhaps even duped him, then he had to smile, she had played her part of Scheherazade to a "t" she had held something back, kept him wanting more. Driving here this evening, thinking about her as he had done for days on end, anticipating their coupling, he had wanted the ultimate. He had wanted her to surrender totally to him. The French called it "the little death" the act of orgasm, that final giving of yourself to another. He had wanted her to give him that prize, to trust him enough to sacrifice herself to him totally while they were locked together as one, while he was inside her. And yet, she had focussed entirely on his pleasure. She had known what she had been doing when she'd ridden him to completion. And here she was, lying next to him, with the concert and the searingly emotional music coming to an end, the strings of the orchestra sublime in their beauty and she had kept that one prize from him. Like Scheherazade, she had left him wanting more. A quote of Shakespeare's came to him like a bolt out of the blue. He hadn't thought of it since school days but it was about Cleopatra and now he remembered thinking he would never meet a woman like that: "age cannot wither her nor custom stale her infinite variety." It might just be, Seb wondered with fascination, that he had met the one woman who could keep him interested. The thought excited him and terrified him in equal amounts.

Chapter Six

BREEZE HAD TOTALLY AVOIDED Seb at work. Hot-desking was one of the company's policies so even though she had an office of her own she could work wherever she chose. She had been astounded Seb hadn't sacked her on the spot when he found she had been scamming him but he obviously knew he had enough of a hold over her for her not to do him any more wrong. At lunch time, instead of eating at her desk as usual, she'd opted ever since that fateful day to take lunch out at one of the many cafes in the square mile.

She loved the City of London, ever changing, history oozing out of the very cracks in the pavement. She could walk the streets that Pepys walked, see where the great fire had started, and marvel at the fabulous buildings designed by Wren, architect of St Paul's Cathedral. Such masterpieces were interspersed by modern structures which made their mark like the gherkin which always reminded Breeze of a massive cigar emerging up and piercing the skyline with such audacity it was even visible from her bedroom window high up on the hills of Crystal Palace. Sometimes on a clear day, she took the lift up to the top floor of Seb's skyscraper headquarters just so she could look in the direction of the house that meant so much to her. It gave her peace to look towards the hills of Crystal Palace and think of her mother reading in the wonderful old conservatory that had been restored with the help of Breeze's previous scam. Her sister grew orchids there, perfect in their symmetry. Her mother deserved the comfort it afforded her, especially after bringing up two girls on her own, and defending them from their father's reckless gambling.

Breeze had scammed in a dozen places, following carefully chosen temp jobs, gathering a thousand here, fifteen hundred there all carefully milked and never had she been discovered. Each time she had found the money to repair a roof or mend the sash windows. Her mother and sister had been so grateful and had admired her so much. Twinges of guilt stung her but she drove them away. She was the only breadwinner in the house and it was a house that had fallen into dire neglect under her father's hand. She had only ever stolen to order, only ever when she had had to, to avoid their home falling around their ears and always she had managed to get away with it. But now, with Seb she had felt the net closing in. Resentment welled up in her but also respect. Not only did he know his company inside out, but he had laid a careful trap for her. The two of them were as resourceful as one another and like a sly fox admiring a rival fox's tactics, she had to admit a sneaking regard for the man who had trapped her.

Breeze wandered down to The Jamaica Wine House in St Michael's Alley. Dating back to 1652 she loved the place with its little mahogany partitions which formed tiny rooms within rooms where she could sit anonymously drinking her coffee. At lunchtime it was murder but taking a late lunch the little booths were quiet. She ordered her coffee and as she waited for it at the bar counter, noticed Richard Waters, Seb's assistant slide into one of the booths, looking around him like a rat scared of a cat. Breeze had never taken to Richard. He followed in Seb's wake and picked up his every word like a beggar snuffling up crusts at a king's table. He had wheedled and engineered himself up the corporate ladder and she had heard rumours of people he had treated badly on the way up. Never a good policy she thought as you may well encounter those people on the way down. Sebastian Dark was intelligent and quick but he couldn't watch every company employee and Breeze had a feeling

Richard had a heart as black as night which he hid from public view.

When, out of the corner of her eye, she caught the rotund figure of Mr Vanhoffer, so recently defeated by Sebastian Dark, she suddenly had a burning desire to know what on earth the unholy alliance of Richard Waters and Mr Vanhoffer could be up to, hidden in the darkness of the booths. She took her coffee and slid silently unseen into the booth adjoining theirs.

'You've got the information for me then, have you, all of it?' asked Mr Vanhoffer.

'Of course I have. That's what we agreed wasn't it? Once this is over, you set me up, like you said you would as Managing Director in your new company and I give you the means to ruin Sebastian Dark's share prices. His company will be a shadow of what it is now by the time we're done. No one must know where this information has come from – you *can* promise me that?' Richard's voice dripped with venom.

'You can rely on me. I want to see Dark ruined and you want to be top of a company rather than playing second fiddle to that bastard. It's a deal made in heaven.'

Breeze craned to listen but her plan was compromised when a large rowdy group arrived celebrating a birthday, drowning out the conversation she was straining to hear. Frustrated, she slipped out of the back entrance and back round to the front. After about ten minutes, Mr Vanhoffer emerged alone, and bumbled off down the street. That was her moment to pounce. Making sure her makeup was pristine, her hair sexily dipping over one eye, she undid her top button and re-entered The Jamaica Wine House sniffing and wiping her eyes with a tissue. Richard was right where she'd expected him, at the bar, ordering a bottle of champagne no doubt to privately toast his newly planned success.

'Hey, Breeze,' he homed in on her like a guided missile.

'What's up?'

It took her only moments to give him some cock and bull story about how Seb had been mean to her, how he'd criticised a report she'd written and made her burst into tears, how she hated his guts. As she knew he would, Richard drank it all in along with three quarters of the bottle of champagne. The more he drank, the more he revealed his treachery. She could see he was on a high as she kept refilling his glass and ordered another bottle, of which she drank only a glass. When she gave him an eyeful of her ample breasts and started running her hand up Richard's thigh, it was only a matter of minutes before he suggested that he finance a hotel room for them both to enjoy a long lunch hour.

'I've fancied you for months, y'know that.'

'Me too,' Breeze had taken the bottle of champagne with them. She pouted her full lips. 'Everyone goes on about how good looking Seb is but I've always thought you're much more intriguing.' Richard could barely stand up by the time they reached the room. He was over her like a rash. She slipped nimbly out of his hands whilst giving him her best come hither smile. 'Come on; let's have just a little more champagne. Then, you can watch me undress.'

She thought his eyes were going to bulge out of his head as he swigged back another glass all in one go, and his tongue crawled out of his mouth as he sat back on the bed and watched her undo her blouse buttons. 'Now,' she encouraged him, 'what was it you were saying about that fucker, Seb?'

'Oh God, don't tell me you're going to talk dirty. I love to talk dirty.'

'I can talk as dirty as you want.' She took a tiny swig from the bottle then handed it to him and watched him gulp it down as if it were mineral water. 'But I want to hear first just how you've stitched up Seb, explain it to me.'

'We're gonna do it in three weeks time, only three weeks

to go b'fore we make our move and Sebastian bloody Dark will be in shit up to his eyeballs.' Richard laughed like all the devils in hell.

Breeze listened carefully, her sharp brain and photographic memory taking everything in. It didn't take long to understand what Richard was up to. She only had to get down to her underwear before, lunging at her unsteadily, Richard crashed to the floor. He knocked himself out on the bedside table and gurgled into unconsciousness. She peered at him as he lay like a slug oozing treachery and snoring like a pig. She knelt down, examined the back of his head, no blood. He'd survive even though he'd have a helluva headache when he came round. So, that's how they were going to do it, she thought as she quickly dressed and cleared out of the hotel room - insider trading. Richard was going to become the illegal eyes and ears of Mr Vanhoffer to bring Sebastian down. She felt a momentary sense of elation. After all, didn't she want to see the man who had trapped her, who had virtually prostituted her for his own ends brought crashing to his knees? But the elation was short lived and born of the sense of injustice she had felt on being found out. She had been stealing tiny amounts from mighty companies for so long and getting away with it that it had hardly felt wrong. Until Sebastian caught up with her.

Her steps were slow, uncertain as she returned to the office, to Sebastian's huge building, the crystal tower to his wealth and power. She looked at the large framed portrait of him which greeted the workers each morning. On first entering that building she had been awestruck by his staggering good looks. The determination in his jawline, the firm lines as he looked seriously out on his great business but she had been left cold by the distance of the man at the top. Then when he had trapped her, she had hated him with a fury. Since then, though, she had seen a different side to him. A vulnerability behind those black beaded eyes and a startling aloneness, the isolation all fabulously wealthy and

42

successful men must feel but rarely show.

For the first time ever, Breeze was in a quandary. One word in Sebastian's ear and she could save him. If she remained silent however, he would go to the wall and all his power over her would disappear. The decision should have been simple. And yet, as she sat down at the computer to perform her proper job, that of earning Sebastian Dark yet more money, she suddenly had no idea which way to turn. Ever since that night when he'd challenged her, all the certainty had disappeared out of Breeze's life. Damn him. Damn Seb Dark. Let Richard and Mr Vanhoffer take him down, what did she care? He could slap her in jail. He should rot in hell for jeopardising the family she had worked so hard to stick together. He had to go. That was it. Decision made. She only had to think up two more evenings filled with the sex - for it was sex and nothing else surely - he craved, to keep Seb ticking over and then he'd have other far more important things to occupy him than her. He'd be fighting for his business life like a drowning man fights to cling on to a piece of wreckage. She couldn't wait.

Chapter Seven

'SO, WHERE IS IT this time?' Breeze felt a twinge of guilt as she settled down next to Seb in his Aston Martin DB9. He looked happy tonight, happy to be with her. 'Or rather where am I taking you as I'm the one who's driving?'

'To the Sharlton Club, St James's Street, off Piccadilly please driver.'

He had picked her up outside the office and was snaking the purring car through the city. 'You look fabulous tonight, Breeze. Your hair's changed, darker isn't it? It suits you. I'd take bets that's nearer to your natural colour. And that outfit's knockout, you make it look timeless.'

Heat jolted through her, right down to her belly as she sat beside him. She smiled; he was nothing if not perceptive. 'In a way it is, it's my mother's she wore it to a society wedding back in the 50s, it's an original Chanel.'

'Hmm a woman of taste. And it looks as fabulous on you today as I'm sure it did then.'

She smoothed down the little flared skirt which sat demurely over her stockinged thighs and undid the buttons on the jacket which made her feel like Lauren Bacall and Audrey Hepburn rolled into one. A white gauze blouse, almost see through challenged the formal lines of the suit, making it instantly sexy. Pearls glistening at her neck nestled alongside the little heart Summer had given her. She wasn't about to tell Seb that she had blown all her available cash on the evening dress she'd worn at the Albert Hall. That she had no other "posh" going out clothes, that her wardrobe contained mainly office clothes. Nor that this suit and pearls that had been given to her mother by her grandfather was one of the last things her mother had preserved to sell in case they were really hard up. Breeze wouldn't ever let her part with such treasures. They came from a happier time before her father had nearly bankrupted the family. Never again would Breeze let them suffer near ruin as they had done then.

'It's sort of appropriate to where we're going, the Sharlton Club requires something demure yet classy, as befits a famous gentleman's club.'

'I'm impressed,' his delectable lips settled into a smile. 'Five minutes around the corner from Buckingham Palace, within a coin's throw of the Ritz. I went there once. I run a charity that gives millions to teenage entrepreneurs from deprived areas and I hosted a lunch there to sweet talk rich grandees out of some of their not so hard earned cash. They looked down their noses at a self made man. Going there with you will be a way of taking them down a peg or two.'

'Excellent.' Breeze stroked the leather of the Aston's seat. Seb was surrounded with luxury, he was discerning and she had thought long and hard over where to take him next. To hear him talk of giving away his money to a charity knocked her off her axis somewhat. He said it matter of factly as if it didn't matter, certainly he kept quiet about it and she had to admit a grudging respect that he didn't shout it from the hilltops like so many other wealthy people did. She thought about all her aspirations when she was a teenager, fledgling businesses that she would have started if only she'd have been given some sort of help and his jawline which had appeared so sharp and unyielding seemed to soften in her eyes.

'But isn't it members only?' Seb said after a moment's thought.

'That's right.'

'Then you're a member?' He looked at her doubtfully; members were all lawyers, captains of industry, MPs, the great and the good although in truth many of them were far from being that.

'Not exactly, but I know how to get in. Trust me.'

He parked the car up and they walked down St James's Street. The area exuded history, the heart of fashionable London. They paused at William Evans, purveyors of country clothing, gun and rifle maker. 'Who nowadays would wear Hunter riding boots, tweed trousers and use walking sticks with handles shaped like affronted looking pheasants waiting to be shot?' joked Breeze.

Seb laughed and put his arm around her to shield her from the evening chill. 'Oh I've met plenty like that at society parties. They bore me silly but they have money to invest.'

At James J Fox, cigar merchant, a city gent wafted cigar smoke into the air and Seb breathed it in. 'Mmm, that's one of life's pleasures I've had to give up since ....'

The word hung on the air. 'Since what?' she asked.

'Oh nothing.' A sudden cloud came over Seb and he rubbed a place on the back of his head, at the base of the skull where she'd seen him put his hand before. When he did, he always gritted his teeth as if he was warding off inner demons, perhaps pain. But he brushed it off, forced a smile and strode on. 'I used to smoke like a chimney; it helped me to get through the stress of buying and selling, kept me calm. But I gave it up just recently. Your pleasures can catch up with you.'

'I guess they can.' Breeze bit her lip and squeezed Seb's hand which lay in hers. He was too private a person to reveal much about himself, but still she wondered whether he was battling something alone which would be much better shared. Then, just as he squeezed her hand in return, she let it fall. She reminded herself that this outing was not for pleasure, and that Sebastian Dark who had a hold over her and was using her for his own ends was not the sort of man ever to get close to. He was ruthless and would discard her once he had what he wanted as surely as he would discard his super smart car when a new model took his eye or his handmade suits when they started to fray. In the story of the thousand and one nights, the King who had a hold over Scheherazade put to death countless wives with whom he became disenchanted and Breeze wasn't going to forget that in a hurry. Sebastian Dark was not the sort of man to whom any right-minded girl, would lose her heart.

Still, as he paced beside her, athletic, virile, strong, she remembered that twinge she had seen on his face, the hand placed to the back of the neck and recalled that she had seen that many times before. It had never meant anything because Sebastian himself had never meant anything to her. Now she found she had begun to scrutinise him more carefully. Why she didn't know. After all, Seb meant as little to her now as ever, didn't he? Maybe it was just that it felt good to be next to such a commanding man, to feel the protection of his broad shoulders. She had never experienced that protection before, had always stood resolutely on her own, battling the world on behalf of her sister and mother, always the strong one, the one who provided. Sebastian knew her darkest secrets, that she stole and lied to get what she needed. But he hadn't shopped her. In an odd twisted way, he had protected her and it felt strangely appealing. It wouldn't last forever, he would tire of her but at least before then Richard and Mr Vanhoffer's plan to ruin him would come into play and then Seb would no longer be a problem because he would be fighting for his financial life. She wanted him to lose his power but she was surprised to find it saddened her as well. Respect, tenderness! Those were the last things she had expected to feel towards Sebastian Dark. She wanted to shake herself to her senses, she must get this evening over with and rush back to her beloved house where she was grounded and had her priorities right.

'Here we are,' she announced in front of anonymous but imposing-looking navy blue doors.

'It's well hidden.'

'Yes, there isn't even a number on the door.' She gave the bell a persistent jab. This place had fascinated her ever since she had waited tables here, way back when she was doing her accountancy exams and dreaming of being self-sufficient and independent. With its boot-scraper at the door and its Victorian streetlamp it was like something out of Sherlock Holmes. The heavy stone steps had been worn to a curve by the booted feet of countless "gentlemen", key members of the establishment, prime ministers and lords who over the decades had come into this hallowed building to plot and scheme the making of kings and the downfall of enemies over glasses of whisky and five course dinners.

'Yes?' The girl at the door was Polish, in a military-style suit, with sharp eyes.

'I am Lady Mary St John. My wedding is booked for here for next February and I want to see the Gladstone Room where the ceremony's being held.'

'I am sorry,' the security girl stood firm. 'I cannot let you in. I haven't been told of any booking to visit the rooms.'

'I don't book when I want to see a venue where I have pledged to spend thousands. You had better let me and my brother in, or I may well investigate other venues. I believe the Athenaeum has rooms just as good ...' Breeze gave her a haughty glance down her nose, playing the consummate aristocrat in her Chanel suit, '... Or even better than yours.'

The girl looked terrified. In the background there were people in overalls running hither and thither carrying huge vases of flowers with worried looks on their faces. They were obviously setting up for a major event that evening and the air was tense. Breeze caught Seb's glance and saw his cheeks dimpled into a smile. He was enjoying her audacity, her bare-faced cheek as she blagged her way in.

'Well, I suppose it won't do any harm.' As soon as the girl hesitated, and moved slightly aside, Breeze swept past her as if she owned the place.

'We'll not be long.'

Breeze clicked confidently in her high heels across the black and white tiled hallway, past the sweeping staircase and straight into the massive Gladstone Room. Seb clunked the door closed behind them and gathered her into his arms. 'You were brilliant, every inch the aristocrat. I just hope you're not going to be too much of a lady now you've conned your way in here.'

Breeze felt the adrenalin pumping through her like the falls at Niagara. He'd made her do this, it was bad, but it was fun and frankly, she thought, as she fell into his long, lingering kiss she had too little fun. And too little excitement. She eyed the door, then noticing the key, flicked it locked. 'We'll have to be quick,' she intoned, sliding her hand down to the already magnificently hard length between Seb's legs. He was rigid, living on the edge, doing things you're not supposed to excited him too. 'They're setting up for a grand dinner. This will be where they come for after dinner drinks. It's all so formal, so proper, doesn't it make you want to roll around on their plush patterned carpet, stick two fingers up at their gleaming crystal chandeliers and fuck like rabbits on their beautiful polished table?'

'Absolutely.' Seb's voice was low, sensuous. 'My God you do choose your places, look at those portraits, Mrs Thatcher, Winston Churchill – what an audience.' He backed Breeze up to a table clothed up in white underneath a mantelpiece literally dripping with fine blossoms. Pale green hydrangeas, heady lilies, white roses, and alstroemerias filled the room with scent. Seb laid Breeze down on the table like an exotic dish at a banquet and stroked his hand tantalisingly over the flimsy gauze blouse. Her heart was already racing with excitement at his touch. His passion for her was something she had come to need desperately. He made her feel sexy, desirable, lusty as he picked at the buttons on her blouse unclothing her and breathing in the perfume between her breasts like a thirsty man drinks at an oasis in the desert. In an instant, he had prised out her breast and was feasting on it hungrily. Feeling the pressure of his toned chest bearing down on her, she knew she wanted him deep inside her. Pulling his shirt out, she ran her fingers over the ridged muscles of his back, feeling him tense with desire at her touch, pulling him to her, onto her. The table was cool and hard beneath her but as he raised her up and held her arse in his hands, pinioned her with his lean body she wanted him, only him. She slipped her hand down to undo him. His length bounced into her hand. It was massive, solid, potent. They had to be quick, but she wanted the moment to last. She raised her legs provocatively then placed Seb's cock over the silk of her panties and started to rub. She was instantly aroused, she started to cream immediately, felt her inner secret place moisten as she used Seb as a sex toy against her throbbing opening. He was still working at her breasts, with one held firmly in his hand. As she worked his cock, used him, he propped her higher on the table. Then, licking his finger, and looking deep into her eyes, he opened the cheeks of her arse and slipped his finger between them to find her G-spot. His finger probed her tightest opening. Sliding just the tip in, she was startled and excited in equal measure. His finger there heightened every sensation, as she forced his cock to press harder through her panties, denying herself the ultimate pleasure of skin against skin but delighting in the wetness oozing over her. The connection with his gaze though made everything more intense, the honesty of his silver flecked eyes staring into hers gave their lovemaking an honesty which touched her heart, intensifying every glorious sensation of his finger pressing into her most secret opening. 'Do you like that?' His breath snagged, 'I can feel you tensing, feel you getting ready for me.'

'It's ... it's scary, but ... don't stop.'

'You make me so hard. Everything about you drives me crazy Breeze. You're the only one who's ever made me feel like this.'

It was too much, too intense, too scary. She had to bring them to completion, had to let him in. Like a harlot, she parted her legs wider, felt him press his finger in just a fraction further, heightening the sensation so that she thought she would come there and then but she didn't want to, didn't want to give herself that totally. But she needed his relief, needed to feel his length. He plunged his cock into her, like a piston firing a high performance car, right up to the hilt; she was so moist, so ready for him. With his finger expertly placed, Breeze had to stare at the stern portraits to stop herself from coming, she wanted to give herself totally to Seb and yet she didn't. That would be too much of a surrender. Still, she felt her hips rise up to meet him, still her heart pounded; still the sweat broke out on her forehead. His digit was causing an ecstasy which spread through her suddenly causing her vision to become blurry, please God he would come first. She wouldn't give herself even though he was almost impossible to resist. His cock was divine, enormous, throbbing with power, he gazed at her, wanting all of her. The table juddered as he drove into her, taking her almost to completion, pounding her, thundering into her, gorgeously, filling her when like a bull stampeding, he groaned and shot his load. She felt satisfaction and triumph and relief that she had held her own orgasm back, that she still had something to tempt him with, that she had still kept some of herself from him. And yet, as he stood, arms rigid against the table, pumping the last remains, emptying himself into her, one part of her wished she could give in totally to him. Wished she hadn't held back. His sandy hair flopped forward and she reached to brush it back. A gesture of tenderness, which he matched by grasping her hand and kissing her palm.

'Spend the night with me.'

It was part command, part a desperate plea. And in that mad instant, her body clamouring for a release she had not allowed herself she heard her voice say, 'Yes. Yes I will.' And her fate was sealed. For, try as she might, she wasn't sure she could resist giving Sebastian Dark the ultimate prize much longer.

It was just as they were doing up the last buttons and Breeze was tidying up her hair that a rap came on the door. 'Looks like we've been found out.' Seb grinned as they made their way to the door and unlocked it. The Polish security girl pursed her lips and looked askance at them as she said, 'Have you and your *brother* quite finished your inspection?'

'Oh yes. Quite.' Breeze stuck her nose up in the air, 'it's just what we wanted.'

As they made their way into the hallway, Seb was enjoying the game and lingered at a political cartoon framed and hung on one of the pillars which depicted two old grandees sitting in the lounge at the Sharlton Club looking at their newspapers.

'Look Mary, this is a classic.'

'Read it to me.' Breeze powdered her nose while the Polish girl looked impatient.

'One of these old guys is saying to the other, "The sex drive of a stoat, the morals of a Tunisian brothel keeper, gentleman, I think our search for a new British Prime Minister is over." That's brilliant don't you think?' Seb let out a full-throated laugh and they finally left the Polish security girl in peace.

Chapter Eight

'I'VE BOOKED US DINNER at the Ritz and then a suite afterwards.'

It was a natural progression from the Sharlton Club to go the five minutes around the corner to the world's most famous hotel. Breeze was wide eyed. 'The Ritz, wow. I've walked past here so many times and peered up at the windows from Piccadilly but I've never been inside. You must have been pretty sure I'd agree to staying the night to have pre-booked. Am I that shallow that you were so certain of me?'

He ushered her past the liveried doorman and through the revolving doors.

'You're not shallow, Breeze, no one could accuse you of that. On the contrary, you're deep, enigmatic. You play all your cards close to your chest. I wish I could get closer but you won't let me.' They walked into mirror-glassed, gold-leaved, rococo splendour where every second step took them under another glittering chandelier.

'Perhaps it's just that I don't have that many aces to play.' She looked at him from under long lashes. 'I think it's you who always holds the strongest hand.'

'I suppose you say that because I'm the one who caught you out. I might appear to have all the power, the money, the status, and the captain of industry tag always attached to my name in the papers. But actually, Breeze, you seriously underestimate your power to fascinate. I loved the Sharlton. You're irreverent and inventive and I'll always remember rutting like rabbits underneath all those stern disapproving

53

portraits.'

'Do rabbits rut?' she asked then blushed as the waiter approached, but if he heard he was too discreet even to raise an eyebrow.

'Mr Dark, it's an honour to have you dining with us tonight.'

Seb motioned to her to sit down on one of the red velvet chairs and she looked around open-mouthed at the extravagant sculpture of reclining gods, the trompe l'oeil Greek gardens painted on the walls and the swags and tails at the window. The Ritz was an explosion of exquisite bad taste which somehow worked perfectly because, like a huge-bosomed bar maid it didn't try to hide how over the top it was.

'You seemed to find that cartoon very funny,' Breeze said as they ordered confit duck ravioli followed by Dover sole and lobster fricassee.

'Oh I did. You see, the thing I value above everything is loyalty, that's the most difficult commodity for a rich and successful man to find. That cartoon was poking fun at the highest in the land. It really struck a chord because it shows that even the most well respected office holders can lack integrity and loyalty. Those characteristics in the people I do business with, and my employees, is the thing I most look for, but it's as elusive as gold dust. I think years of discovering how difficult it is to find is one of the things that has made me jaded, made me lose my faith in people, almost.'

Breeze had been enjoying her starter but suddenly it tasted like cardboard in her mouth. She thought of Richard and Mr Vanhoffer and their vile secret that she knew. The three of them, her included were like vipers trying to sting Sebastian. Did she really want to be part of that? She was trying hard to hate Seb as she had when he'd first exposed her but somehow she couldn't any longer. He talked animatedly; jokes came quickly to him when he was relaxed like this. She couldn't take her eyes off features which had once seemed steely and sharp but in reality had a softer side. She liked the strong Roman nose, the glittering eyes with their shards of lively silver and the blonde lights in his hair which had felt so soft under her fingers and which she ached to touch again. She realised she was looking forward to their night together. She wanted him to hold her close, to make love to her. She ate only half her main course before closing her knife and fork and saying, 'Seb, how hungry are you?'

He stopped mid-forkful, and his smile made her melt. 'Why? Are you thinking of perhaps taking desert in our room?'

'Absolutely. A special sort of desert.' She put down her serviette and allowed him to escort her out of the blousy dining room and into the privacy of their suite. The Royal Suite was sumptuous, split-level, a curious oval shape. As she looked out at the night settling over Green Park, she felt Sebastian caress her from behind. He ran kisses up her neck distracting her from the plane trees spreading their branches over lovers escaping arm in arm from the madness of Hyde Park Corner into the sanctuary of the green oasis. The scent of newly cut grass wafted upwards as Sebastian's arms enclosed her, pressing her against the gym-toned sleekness of his chest. She turned to him, and felt her body tingle as he undressed her. His eyes delved into her soul as he carefully undid her clothing, peeling it away. She stood naked before him and watched, the round globes of her breasts rising and falling, his slow undressing. When he stepped towards her and cleaved his body to hers it sent ripples of pleasure through her like the first rumblings of an earthquake. When he lay her down and ran his fingers over her body from her toes, up her ankles, over her calves, kissing her skin with hungry passion, she buried her fingers in his hair and luxuriated in its softness. When he mounted her, she wrapped her legs around him with an abandon that said more eloquently than words, 'I need you.' As he cupped her

55

breasts in his hands, as she saw his eyes flicker with ecstasy as she grasped the rock hardness between his legs and guided him into her, she realised she had come to a decision. He was going to make love to her, to sleep a full night with her and this time she wanted him. All of him. All her life she had been told to be independent, to be an island but she didn't want to be the Ice Queen any more. This man was special. Coupling with him, giving herself to him was the ultimate. It might destroy her. He might decide that having won the final prize he would discard her, throw her to the wolves, leave her behind. But sometimes she reasoned as she teased open her petals and guided him inside, you had to take risks. Sometimes it was worth it.

Sebastian raised himself up to kneel on the bed with her locked over the magnificence of his cock. He brought his arms around her, his muscles sinewy as he lifted her onto him, as she slid down the enormity of him. Her hair fell forward, and he breathed in the scent of it. 'Come for me, Breeze, come over me, come inside me, give me everything.' Her whole body was welded on to him, gloriously trapped in his hold, his cock like a ramrod filled her and tantalised her. He grabbed her buttocks and started lifting her up and down so that the sensation of his ridged cock sliding over her aching clit, massaging the little bud to sensitivity was heaven. Breeze threw her head back and he closed his mouth over her nipple, so softly, so carnally she could hear his lips doing their work as he licked and flicked with his tongue. Her clit swelled like a ripe red cherry. Every piston movement of his cock made her wetter, as he drove faster, her heart racing to keep up.

'You're gorgeous, I need you, I want to fuck you forever,' he breathed in her ear. 'I want to drive you wild, hear you cry out for more.' His voice as smooth as milk chocolate lilted like a chant as she closed her eyes in sheer abandonment, giving herself up to his driving force. So this was what being ravished really meant, it meant having every sinew of your being focussed on one man, being possessed, being ... Red hot desire moulded his muscles into relief. He had leant down, without her even seeing it and now, as he eased her forward slightly off his burgeoning cock, she felt a vibration so delicious, so unexpected, so wildly exhilarating it forced goose bumps racing up her skin. The vibrator was small, discreet, he played it just long enough on her ripe clit to practically drive her up through the ceiling. He threatened to melt her under his red-hot gaze. then he switched it to the shaft of his cock. Instantly he hardened and swelled inside side her filling her totally. Then, like a magician pulling a dove out of a hat, he started to bounce her and as he did, he tantalised her with the vibrator, moulding it onto her clit with such exquisite pressure she knew she couldn't hold herself much longer. Rising, upwards and downwards in a mounting rhythm, her eyes seeing stars, her luscious come juice trickling over his prick, her breasts bouncing up and down in his face, he urged her on. He breathed, his voice reaching her as if they were floating in space, 'That's it, Breeze fuck me, fuck me good. Come over me, let me feel you lose it.' That did it, that brought her over the hill. His filthy words, his total abandon, his pounding cock relentlessly driving her up and down, the vibrator deliciously tantalising her cunny made her explode, forced her to come in sensational jolting pulses. Breeze let out a scream and a long aching sigh as her orgasm rode him again and again, the sweat beading on her brow, her whole body pulsating like a softly purring machine. The first time, the first time she had ever given herself fully with him inside her and the relief, the blessed relief felt like being reborn.

Breeze collapsed on the bed, floated downwards, felt as if her whole body were swimming in warm water. It was sublime, it was beautiful, it was the ultimate. She realised in that moment that he hadn't been looking selfishly to win the prize ... but that he had given her the prize, the ability to totally let go, to abandon yourself to another. In that

57

moment, regarding Seb gazing down at her looking more content than any man she had ever seen, stroking her damp forehead, she knew she was falling inexorably, inexplicably for him. She hadn't wanted to, she didn't understand it but she was. That was her last thought before she fell into a slumber so perfect, she gave herself up to the warmth of his arms and the sigh of his lips.

When she woke it was to see dawn play in peaches and burnished gold across the tips of the trees waving outside in Green Park. The night had seemed so perfect, but the morning after was spiked with reality. Breeze looked at Seb slumbering, narrow hips wrapped in a sheet. Even at rest, the muscles rounded like a range of hills. In his sleep, his hand went to the back of his head and he winced. If things had been normal, if they'd had a proper relationship she'd have woken him, questioned him about that pain – for pain it must be that plagued him in sleep. But things weren't normal. They weren't honeymooners, they weren't a happy ever after; they were two people thrown together by circumstances. Maybe they were simply misfits who had shared something extraordinary but whose time was coming to an end. Next week was his birthday and was bound to be their last time together. Seb was famous for being a loner, he would revert to type; they always did. He looked perfect hero material now but she decided she'd rather leave with that impression of him on her senses than have him wake, see the coldness return to his eyes, realise that she was just one more conquest in a life filled with conquests. That now he'd had the ultimate from her, spent the night with her, she would be expendable. He'd keep her, might use her one more time, after all she was his birthday present to himself and then she'd be discarded. Still, she thought as she looked at his deeply slumbering form and picked up her clothes to sneak away. It had been good. Very, very good. No, not just that. It had been sensational.

She raced through the park, towards Victoria Station, and

remembered that she still hadn't told him of Richard's treachery. She'd still retained one bit of power, she still had the ability to save Seb or see him go to the dogs. Her independence told her to keep that bit of ammunition up her sleeve, but time was running out. If she didn't tell him soon, he could be ruined. She made it home, her head spinning. Her mother's exhortations to always be independent, her father's ability to pursue his own ends whilst recklessly ignoring his family dogged her. But how long should she hang on to her mother's experience and make it hers? Her history was her own to mould. When she got back, she needed to think. A jog around Crystal Palace Park always made her see more clearly. She'd go the long way today. Her body, moreover her soul needed the solace of a good long run.

She pounded the streets, then the paths and finally the grass breathing in the cleansing air as if it were wine. She'd got herself into such a mess. Being a thief, for that's what she was, had been a move of desperation, then it had been too easy to carry on. And look where it had got her? Enthralled to a man who would squash her like an insect once he had done with her. Any thoughts that he might have any emotional attachment to her was surely an illusion. Her steps slowed as she approached home. But as she did, she saw Summer and her mother standing at the window looking for her. Something had happened, she was always on edge, had always taken care of them. She bounded up the steps. But when she got in they were beaming.

'You've just missed him.' Her mother had a cooling pot of coffee on the table, cups were arranged around it. Expensive chocolate biscuits which they only brought out on special occasions lay half eaten on a plate.

'Missed who?' Breeze's hackles were raised.

Summer tucked a lock of hair behind her ear. 'Sebastian Dark himself. He's so much better looking than his photographs in the papers. And that car.' Summer almost swooned. 'You must have done something pretty major to be that much in the boss's good books that he'd go to the trouble of coming here.'

'I showed him around,' Breeze's mother said proudly, clearing away the cups. 'He has hidden depths that man. He's interested in Victorian and Edwardian architecture, was very knowledgeable, in fact. He was most impressed with your grandfather's designing of the house. And he loved how you'd restored the old conservatory. He was very admiring of Summer's orchids, said he'd seen some like them when working in the far east. He congratulated us on such a beautiful house. No, "home", that was the word he used. "You have a beautiful home, Mrs Monaghan, I envy you that. No amount of money can make that happen." I told him it was all down to you, that we would have lost your grandfather's house years ago without your hard work.'

'What on earth was he doing here?' Her mother was such a sensible woman. Breeze had never seen her looking like that, sort of besotted. Seb must have turned the charm full on.

'He said you must have lost this in the office,' said Summer dropping the gold heart with the little diamond into her hand. 'He was passing by so he dropped it in. He noticed you always wear it and might be worried about losing it. That's so thoughtful for a busy man. I thought you said he was mean and selfish. Just goes to show you never can tell. Oh, and he also left this padded envelope. Something boring to do with work he said.' Summer breathed in the air, 'I can still smell his aftershave, just like pine forests.' The two women were still singing his praises as her mother and Summer, invigorated by their visitor and glowing in his praise went off to water the orchids. Breeze collapsed onto a dining room chair, trailed the little heart and chain in her fingers then opened the envelope. Inside was a long box and inside that laying on a blue velvet bed, the prettiest necklace she had ever seen. A string of sublime fire opals, glowing and changing in the sunshine. She had never seen opals like that before, their lights danced on the skin of her hand. She read the card inside. She was intrigued at the large, swirly, extravagant handwriting. Surely, Seb's father had been wrong when he said his son wasn't artistic, that handwriting and his eye for colour in choosing the beautiful opals belied that. More like Seb had never been given the chance to express that side of himself. *'Breeze, I wanted to say thank you. I bought these at the jewellers at the Ritz. They're unique, just like you. x'*

Breeze held their coolness which reminded her of the coolness of his fingers on her skin. It was gorgeous. She couldn't accept it of course. For what did it represent? How he had callously bought her sexual favours. Still, she tried the opals around her neck. They suited her perfectly. But would suit her even better if she coloured her hair back to her original colour, rich chestnut. It would feel good to be her real self again, for in a way he was the one person in the world from whom she no longer had anything to hide. He had seen her at her worst, had caught her stealing. And he had seen her at her most vulnerable, when she had laid herself before him and surrendered totally to his masculinity, trembling at his touch. If only their weird and artificial relationship didn't prevent him from seeing her at her best. For she did have a best side, loyal, nurturing. Even the sex which had been fabulous, mind-blowing wasn't entirely her. It had been a power game never a love match. The word jolted her. Love. Saturday, his 30th birthday must be their last coupling. Love wasn't something she could consider in the same moment she thought about Seb, for if she ever fell in love with a man like him, and he rejected her, it would destroy her.

But one thing she was finally sure of as she made her way upstairs to get washed and dressed was that she could not hate him any more. And that was why as soon as she was ready she was going to go right out, and tell him about the vile, underhand plot his closest aide was hatching to destroy him.

Chapter Nine

'MR DARK CAN'T BE disturbed. He's working on something very important right now.' His secretary guarded him with a loyalty that was steadfast. That's the way people were around Seb Dark. He inspired it in them.

'I'm sorry,' Breeze marched past the secretary and barged in. It was now or never.

Seb looked astounded to see her; she had kept her distance from him in the office so well of late. 'It's OK, Mrs Hammond,' he waved the concerned woman away. 'I'm happy to see Miss Monaghan any time.'

'Thank you.' Breeze sat, only the flimsy barrier of the desk stood between them. She yearned to reach out and touch him, like you would a magnificent panther. She thought she saw a flicker of the same response in him. But this was business, not pleasure. 'There's something I've been meaning to tell you for a while. I ... I held back. I'm sorry, because it makes me look as bad as them, when I'm not, really I'm not.'

'You're talking in riddles, Breeze.' His sensual mouth firmed. She felt her legs weaken, her fingers fluttered to her throat as if she wanted to still the pulse which now raced every time he was near.

'It's about Richard, and Mr Vanhoffer. You may not believe me. I hardly even know where to begin.' She found she was stuttering; he looked so devastatingly handsome. Now she had relinquished the protection of hating him she was drawn to him like a magnet.

'Then begin at the start, it's always easiest.'

63

She poured out to him what she knew, how she knew it. She could see in the tight lines of his sensual mouth that one question lay unanswered – why she had taken so long to tell him? She only hoped to God it wasn't too late.

He steepled his fingers, a signet ring, one he had said had been given to him by his father, the father who never valued his work but whom he still honoured, shone on his finger. 'I admire you in coming here today, Breeze. I wondered how long it would be before you told me. You see, I already knew.'

Breeze felt the floor whoosh from under her, like she was in a fast moving lift. 'You knew?'

He smiled, a smile that didn't reach his eyes. 'Yes, I knew. It turns out that even I have a heart and on reflection I felt sorry for Mr Vanhoffer. Even though I took over everything he owned, I respected him as a smart man of business. So I made him an offer. An extremely generous offer to come and work for me, helping behind the scenes to pull ailing companies out of the mire. But I didn't tell anyone else I'd taken him on. He informed me a while ago that Richard had approached him. And I told him to string Richard on. I needed to know what he was up to. It confirmed some things about Richard's lack of loyalty I had already heard on the grapevine but couldn't prove. Richard will be getting his marching orders today. He's got a wife and a young family. I shan't be taking it any further for his sake. I simply hope he's learnt his lesson.'

'You're very generous.'

'For a bastard you mean. Isn't that how you've seen me?'

'I ... well, maybe. At times.'

'I understand how money drives people to do bad things. Integrity's a difficult talent to achieve in this business but I do my best.'

He did, he so did. In that moment, she wanted to have him take her in his arms, to hold her like he'd done so many times before. But now, he didn't move towards her. A dark lack of liveliness dulled his eyes. Had she failed him so comprehensively? Like so many other people had done? She wished she'd come earlier. Wished she hadn't thought so badly of him that she'd waited.

'And now, I'm sorry, Breeze, I have many papers I have to wrap up, things I have to complete before–' He stopped mid sentence as if catching himself out. For one moment, she thought he was going to reach out and stroke her like he had so many times before. Electricity crackled between them. Then died, as if he'd flicked a switch. His voice was flat. 'We're still on for Saturday? Your last obligation to please me.' Still there was the heat of desire, but also a holding back which she didn't understand.

'So, it will be the last then?' She felt it difficult to swallow. The last. He was going to let her go. The very real thought that she might never enjoy his caresses again made her world implode; she desperately wanted to reach out and feel those muscles tense under her fingers again, see those eyes flicker as she took him in her hands. But his stiff stance signalled that this was not the appointed time and place. His steely control won over the sparks of desire that lit his eyes. She bit her lip.

'Yes, don't look so serious. I will be releasing you from our business deal. And there will be no police, no jail, you've paid your price.'

Somehow, now it didn't feel like a price paid. She'd been spared but she also felt bereft. As the door closed, and the lift carried her down, there were a million things she'd left unsaid. And there was also the necklace in her pocket which she'd planned to give back. Somehow she couldn't bear to let it go. At least they had Saturday.

Chapter Ten

BREEZE HAD PLANNED THE last Saturday to be at the House of Lords. He'd like the irreverence of fornicating in a place which prided itself on its formality – in his own way he was as much of a rebel as she was. She had phoned to tell him the place and time but unusually had got his answerphone. She had left a message and now, here she was standing in the street at the entrance of the Houses of Parliament which lead to the Cholmondeley Room. And he was late. Seb had never been late before.

She waited and waited, paced up and down, wore a groove in the pavement, watched the afternoon turn to evening. No way would Seb willingly have stood her up. He was a man who kept his word, something must be wrong.

In desperation she took a taxi to headquarters and almost ran up to his office. It was deserted. Maybe, she clung on to a small ray of hope, the security man, Ronald would know something. He knew everything and everybody.

By the time she reached him, she was panting. 'Hey, Miss Monaghan, don't you look a pretty picture. And your hair, you've coloured it down. If you don't mind my saying it matches your eyes perfectly. I always did think you was pretty striking as a blonde but brunette's much more the real you. You must be going somewhere mighty fine lookin' so good.'

'I was,' she had thought up various stories about why she needed to know where Seb lived then realised she did that out of habit. Why did she always have something to hide? It was time to be honest. 'I was actually meeting Mr Dark. He and I have been seeing each other for some weeks now.'

'Oh, Miss Monaghan I'm so pleased. You two would make a lovely couple and that man needs a good woman.'

'The thing is, Ronald, he never turned up like we agreed. I ... I'm worried about him, I can't get him on the phone either.'

The security guard's brow furrowed, his face full of concern. It was typical of Seb that he should inspire such concern. 'Have you been to his apartment?'

'We never went there; we've always gone out to places. Look, Ron, I know it's breaching confidentiality but I'm really worried about him. Do you know where he lives? Could you give me the address?'

'I know you work as hard for Mr Dark as anyone. I've seen you in here enough, burning the night oil. Of course I know where he lives. His chauffeur and I are like that.' He crossed his fingers into a knot. 'Here, this is where you need to go.'

Heart pounding, a sick puddle in her stomach at what might be wrong, Breeze thought of the headaches from which Seb suffered. She'd suspected it was just stress, but perhaps he was more ill than he let people know. Please God it wasn't something really serious. Breeze jumped in a taxi. The address was in St Katharine's Dock, nestling next to the Thames within sight of the Tower of London. It was a bustling marina full of bars, and restaurants and some very lucky people had chosen to live there on boats at the exclusive moorings. As she approached, there was a frisson of drama. An ambulance, lights flashing. Suddenly she saw Seb at the centre of it, shaking hands with a paramedic, slapping another on the back. They talked earnestly to him before wishing him well and departing. Breeze ran, until she thought her chest would burst with the effort, and crashed onto the scene just as Seb waved goodbye to the paramedics. She ran to be face to face with him, her carefully curled hair now wild about her cheeks, her white lace cocktail dress contrasting with the fire opals at her neck. As she gasped for breath she didn't even care that she looked a state.

'Where have you been?' she shrilled, 'I've been terrified, I thought all sorts of things had happened to you. Why didn't you phone?'

He gave her that steely stare she was so used to. His eyes bored into her, black as the night. Oh my God, she had so misjudged this situation. She put her hand to her mouth, suddenly feeling sick. She had panicked, run wildly to him as if they were lovers and now she would be spurned. Cast off. How could she have overreacted so when she meant so little to him? Her heart leapt to her mouth, her face lost its animation and she made to turn away. He was just her boss. Nothing more. Even their arrangement for no strings sex was over. All was dust and despair. She wished the ground would open and swallow her whole. It wasn't her place to care about him. She meant nothing to him.

As she turned her back and real tears pricked the back of her eyes she felt a hand on her shoulder. 'Breeze, come back. I'm sorry I worried you, really I am.'

As she turned, a new light softened his features. Was he sorry for her – heavens she didn't want his sympathy, didn't want him to know that she had fallen for him, that deep in her heart she needed him, desired him, missed him, thought of him every minute of every day. When surely to him, she was just a quick screw on a Saturday night.

'You did worry me.' She fought hard to hold back the tsunami of emotion that threatened to engulf her. There, she had shown him she cared. 'What on earth has happened? What was the ambulance doing here? Why didn't you tell me something was up? I waited hours for you.' She bit her lip and quietened down, people were watching. A lover's tiff they shrugged and smiled as they went by.

'Are you trying to tell me you actually care for me?' His words were soft, as if he almost dare not say them.

She sniffed. She would NOT cry. 'Oh, you fool,

Sebastian, of course I do. More than that I was terrified, I thought maybe you'd been in an accident or something. You're normally so damned reliable with every wretched thing you do, you were meant to be with me.'

As soon as she said it, she didn't know what had hit her. Instead of walking away, instead of rejecting her and leaving her his arms came about her like the protective wings of an eagle, warm and strong, holding her hard, so hard the breath was squeezed out of her. Towering above Breeze, Seb looked down and lifted her chin. 'Could you not, just for once, Breeze, accept that maybe I feel the same way about you? That for ages I've been fascinated by you. Maybe it's just time we started trusting each other. Maybe it's about time we said what we really think because I ... adore ...' His gaze searched her face, those gorgeous eyes silver and grey, pierced her heart. She held her breath and the whole world condensed into the tiny spot of land where they stood, the earth had stopped, her heart waited to beat, '... you. I adore you.'

She couldn't believe those words, but as his lips met hers, as he sought her out, sank into her, supported her on legs which had lost the power to stand, wrapped her in his warmth she knew she had to believe. She had to trust and be trusted, as she closed her eyes and felt him take her to heaven. Their kiss seemed to last a lifetime. When he released her she felt she had dreamed it. But no, this was Seb, and he was taking her by the hand. 'Come on to my boat and I'll explain everything.'

He took off his jacket and draped it over his shoulder. He looked totally gorgeous now, slightly ravaged and unkempt. He sat her down inside the luxury motor cruiser, took a seat beside her and put his hand to his forehead. Every move made her heart lurch. This incredible man was in love with her, the world had shifted on its axis. 'That ambulance came here in the early hours of the morning. I've been having trouble with headaches, really severe ones. I've been for tests and they'd told me there was nothing they could do. That the tumour threatened to be terminal. I did everything I could, ate a special diet, gave up smoking tried all sorts of quack remedies. You do when you're desperate like that. Then I gave in, lost all my drive, tried to tell myself I was bored with life.' She squeezed his hand, she wasn't hearing this. 'That was ages ago before you and I ... That was why you've been so important to me Breeze. I'd grown disillusioned with life itself. Even before I became ill, it had sort of left me behind. I'd achieved everything I set out to but when I became ill it made me realise with all my wealth in reality I had nothing of value. No one would have given a damn when I went, if I'd gone. Then, you came along. And changed everything.'

'But what about ...' She couldn't say the word tumour, it sounded so ugly.

'I had pains this morning so bad, as bad as they've ever been. Some weeks ago they'd given me a new drug to try out, something that's only trialling, something that's not even on the market yet. When the pains came ...' He touched the back of his head in that old familiar place. '... It scared the hell out of me. I thought that was it. But then, when they got me to the hospital and under the scanner. Well, they said the tumour is shrinking. Something's happened, Breeze. It's got smaller. It's going. I don't know whether it's the new drug or maybe something else in my life,' there was a subtle change in the air, a lightness as he regarded her. He couldn't possibly mean that she had had something to do with this. 'I finally have something to fight for. All I know is it's got to be the best birthday present I've ever had.'

Breeze listened as if she was sitting in the middle of a tornado, or riding on a rollercoaster. 'Oh no, I never wished you happy birthday.' She didn't know whether to laugh or cry. And I bought you a present and I left it, I don't know where, I've been rushing around like a mad thing. You know something?' She smiled. 'It doesn't matter what's making you better. All that matters is, you're here and you're going to be here a lot longer.'

'No,' he said, holding her face in his hands. 'What matters is that you're still with me.'

With that, he took her hand and led her into the bedroom. It was as if he was preparing her for a slow, erotic Argentine tango. She held her breath as he reached behind her and slid the zip down her back. Fingers fluttering over the surface of her skin, over her shoulder blades – she was alive, dazzling under his touch. He combed his hands through her hair and breathed in the scent of fresh shampoo and French perfume. She gasped as he traced her lips with the pad of his thumb. Slowly, slowly he moved. He was the master of this delicate dance.

His high cheekbones shadowed in the half-light. Suddenly Breeze had no more fear or reservations. She was no longer playing a part. She was his. She desperately tore the shirt from him and flung it to the floor. He was dense-packed muscle, whipcord strength. His hands grasped the delicate lace of her dress and shimmied her trembling body free of it. Her white underwear was virginal, pure, the lacy bra revealing darkly shadowed areolas. His hand came to caress her heavy mounds. His touch sent sparks of heat through her aching body. This was what she wanted – to be possessed completely. But first to possess him. Stilling his hands, she sank to her knees before him, undid the button on his trousers, whiplashed the belt from his waist and tossed it on the bed. She took him in her hands; he was all solid strength and length. He looked down at her from a height and cupped her head in his hands, directing her onto the spear of hardness between his legs. As she wrapped her lips around the tip of his cock, she delighted in the musky saltiness, the ultimate maleness of him. Placing one hand at the base and massaging his balls, she used the other to tease him into her mouth.

He sighed as he gripped her hair, moaned as she flicked her tongue up and over the sensitive ridges of his cock, groaned as she used her swift hand, her mouth, her whole being to bring him pleasure immeasurable. Her head bobbed up and down, the rhythm driving him mad. She wanted to give him so much, to give him everything. She saw the hills and valleys of muscle in his thighs tense, heard his breath pant hard, felt him grip her hair in his hands and then, gloriously, he spilt his load. She drank him in, enjoying the sensation of his being totally in her thrall. Of him losing himself to her.

He lifted her up, poured her a glass of wine and watched with hungry eyes as she lay on the bed drinking it. She was already tipsy at the sight of him, the smell of him, the taste of him. Gentle waves lapped the side of the boat. A light breeze caused the masts of neighbouring yachts to whistle in the night air. The sounds of the city rushing by outside meant nothing to them in their cocoon. Here they were alone. Seb lay her back and started massaging her feet, his gentle caress sending little shivers through her legs. When he kissed the hollow at the back of her knees, her senses shot into overdrive. When he lay alongside her, he was so beautiful she could hardly believe he was all hers. Like a Greek God, like a Roman Statue come alive she couldn't keep from staring at him. Breeze's fingers caressed his firm round buttocks, delighting in the roughness of his skin, so different to hers. He was already hard for her again, ready to drive her wild. He took the bottle of wine. 'You look absolutely stunning in white lace, but …' a wicked glow burnt in his eyes, 'I need you naked for what I'm about to do next.' He unflipped the catch of her bra, slid her panties off then stood to grab the bottle of wine again. She gasped. In the confines of the boat he looked even more enormous, even more potent. He knelt beside her and trickled a trail of wine over her stomach then bent and licked it out of her navel. The sensation uncurled a secret place in her belly, a snaking anticipation building. She knew what was next. Her nipples cried out for attention and when he sprinkled the sharp sweet wine over them, he caught it with his tongue, lapped all around her sensitised breasts. She wanted him more; she wanted to drive him crazy.

Like a harlot, she clutched her breasts and offered them to him. When he moistened them with more of the nectar-like liquid she pulled him up to kneel before her and thrust his cock between her mountainous breasts. Driven mad, he pumped the channel of her breasts while she squeezed them hard, watching his cock burgeoning between them. He was so massive now, she was finally ready for him and she didn't want him coming too soon. She thrust him down between her legs, opened them wide, raised herself up to receive him and felt him plunge inside her. Filling her massively, never had he felt so huge. The odour of wine and sweet perspiration scented their coupling. Breeze clasped his buttocks driving him into her, she felt the thick glory of his cock riding her clit, so smoothly. She gripped him tightly never wanting it to end, feeling the orgasm start small in the pit of her core, expanding with each rise and fall. 'More, more, harder,' she cried. He was like a high speed train, like a space rocket, like a stallion serving a mare. He drove into her, faster and faster, harder and harder until she cried out with the ultimate explosion of a massive orgasm as she felt inside her, Seb's magnificent cock firing off as his erection came to thundering fruition. They rode the wave together, like surfers in the ocean, perfectly in time, perfectly in harmony, perfectly exhausted, perfectly spent. Perfectly at one.

'Breeze,' Seb said, as he finally got back his breath, 'promise me you'll never leave. Promise me this isn't our last night. Make it our first.'

She leant over, combed her fingers through his hair and said, 'I'm happy to throw in my lot with you, happier than I've ever been.'

'And promise me one other thing.'

She smiled, her sensuous lips so broad she wondered if she'd ever stop smiling. 'Anything,' she said.

'Never be blonde again, never be someone you aren't.' He teased chestnut curls through his fingers.

'For you I'll do anything,' she said and with that, she raised her glass and toasted, 'Happy birthday,' as she folded herself into his loving arms again.

Out of Focus
by Primula Bond

Chapter One

'THIS IS THE EXACT style I've been looking for. Classic, but quirky. I particularly like the monochrome. Where can I find the artist?'

Eloise glanced across from her perch in the corner and pushed her glasses up her nose. 'That's me. I mean, these are my pictures.'

The man kept his gaze on the central photograph. It was of Jake in a deserted department store at night, taken from behind so none of the punters would recognise him. He was butt naked, lit by a single spot, and being jostled by fully-clothed mannequins.

'What I want is for you to come to my place and take a portrait of my tribe,' the man said, turning to look at her. He had burning blue eyes and sleek black hair greying at the temples. A modern day Dracula. 'I should warn you. We are more like the Addams family. But I want to create the illusion that we're normal. Beautiful. Capable of sitting still for five minutes.'

'Sounds intriguing. I'll just check my appointments.' Eloise flicked through the pages of her totally empty diary.

He was suddenly standing right in front of her. 'I forgot to say. The sitting needs to be done this weekend before they all scatter to the four winds.'

Eloisa remembered her manners and stood up. Up close he was even taller. She guessed that his suit was expensively tailored but his red silk tie was very slightly loosened, giving him a rakish air.

He noticed that she was staring at his undone top button. 'Do excuse me. It's been a tough day. Cedric Epsom.'

'Eloise Stokes.'

He took her hand.

'So, Eloisa Stokes, may I commission you to take the family portrait?'

'It's Eloise.' She expected him to shake her hand, but instead he lifted it and brushed it across his upper lip. He seemed to be smelling her skin as if her hand was a posy. Or a morsel he was about to devour. She went hot all over. He kissed her fingers as they crooked into a fist. Was that the tip of his tongue bumping over her knuckles? She had the weirdest urge to push her fingers hard into his mouth and have him suck them one by one …

He gave her back her hand as if they'd just finished some kind of archaic dance. 'So it's a date. For Friday?'

'Yes. Sure. Fantastic.' Stammering like an amateur.

He walked towards the door, then turned and handed her his card. 'Come by my office in half an hour. I never do business without discussing payment first.'

Eloise watched him walk down the street, snapping back his French-cuffed wrist to check his watch. Jake emerged from his office. Normally he would hover, keep tabs on everything that was going on in the gallery. But now he was marching about switching off the main lights unnecessarily sharply. He left one bright spot illuminating her picture of him.

'Did you hear that amazing conversation, Jake? My first professional assignment, and from passing trade, too. How about that!'

Jake locked the gallery door.

'I'd hardly call Cedric Epsom passing trade.'

'You know that guy?'

'Everyone knows him!' Jake gave a sardonic laugh.

'He's a kind of modern day Machiavelli. You know, patron to the arts. Well connected, too. I mean, everyone from Clinton to Clintwood comes through his door when they're in London. So if he likes it, buys it, and hangs your work in his house, it will be seen by all the movers and shakers–'

Eloise lifted her long hair to cool her neck and gave a wriggle of excitement. 'So why are you stamping about looking like thunder? Doesn't this make me your star protégée? After all, you discovered me first!'

He pulled her away from the window and took hold of her. She leaned into him, pushing her big breasts against his shirt and rubbing them slowly against him, just the way he liked it. The breasts she kept hidden under loose tunics and had only ever unwrapped for him. His mouth fell open as her nipples pricked hard through the soft fabric.

'I just wish it wasn't him, of all people. He eats women for breakfast, Elle.'

'He's old enough to be my father.' She slapped gently at his cheek. 'This is a commission, for God's sake, not a casting couch. My chance to get myself on the map! I'm not a kid, Jake. And I'm hardly a Playboy centrefold. He's posing for me, remember, not the other way round. I'm in total control–'

'You don't know the half of it!' Jake slammed her against the wall, his breath hot and angry on her face. The blow buzzed through her bones. 'You're a brilliantly talented photographer, Elle, I've made sure of that. But you're still so naïve! Christ, you've never even fucked another man!'

'And? What are you now, my lord and master?' She tried to shake him off, but his fingers dug into her skin through the thin shirt and he pushed his knee between her legs and up, so that her pussy was grinding against his thigh. She was breathing hard now, but the fury was shafting through her body, making it spark with a toxic heat. 'Well, maybe now's the time to start!'

He pushed her shirt up to reveal her big breasts encased in a silky pink bra. He cradled them as he liked to do, flicking his thumbs across the tightening nipples.

'Cocky words like that don't suit you. You're mine, Eloise Stokes. And you always will be.'

The heady sensation as he tweaked her hot nipples while she tried to fight him was too strong. She struggled weakly. 'How could I be only yours? I'm 22. There's a whole world waiting for me out there!'

And the world was walking home past the window right now, sweaty from the heatwave that was sucking London dry.

'I taught you everything you know.' He pinched harder, watched her head fall back against the wall. 'So I think you should be thanking me, don't you?'

She gritted her teeth, gathering every ounce of strength she had to resist temptation. Then she pushed him away and pulled down her shirt.

'Of course I'm grateful to you. I'm proud that I can call myself a professional now. But I'm not going to grovel on my hands and knees.'

'Shame. Perhaps we should try that next time!' He laughed, reached for her again. 'But you still know you won't get anywhere without my guidance.'

Eloise wrenched open the door before she gave in to him again. Relished the warm breeze blowing over her skin. 'Just you watch me.'

Chapter Two

HALF AN HOUR LATER she was stepping out of a lift on the penthouse floor of Cedric Epsom's corporate building. The City was spread out like a baking feast, the Docklands railway trundling lethargically around the glittering skyscrapers.

Inside the office there was nothing so pedestrian as a computer or telephone to be seen, or even any other people. Just a huge glass desk the size of her kitchen, a vase of lilies big enough to bathe in, and an array of Dom Perignon bottles lined up on a chrome bar.

Cedric had taken his jacket and tie off by now, but somehow the open collar and sleeves rolled up over his powerful arms made him look more scary, not less. He showed her to a white leather chair by the window and handed her a glass of champagne. The first delicious sips lulled her into a kind of welcoming helplessness.

'So, Eloisa Stokes.'

'It's Eloise, Mr Epsom.'

'Prettier this way. It can be my special name for you.'

Label, more like, she thought, holding the cold bubbles on her tongue for a moment. *I bet you like to label all your people and possessions.*

'So. Let's get the finances out of the way so we can both relax.' He sat on the edge of the desk, swinging one long leg. She finally understood what a master of the universe looks like in the flesh. 'Because by the time you come over to Richmond I want us to be, well, better acquainted.'

His eyes were chips of blue ice. His gaze never left her

face as they started negotiating her fee for the shoot. She wondered if this intense attention, scrutiny almost, was part of his business technique. Because it was certainly working. She felt hot, bothered, and drawn to him like a magnet.

She accepted a second glass of champagne, plucked a figure out of the air as they talked, then doubled it.

'Done!' He smacked his hands down on his thighs. 'I hope this is going to be the start of a very lucrative partnership, Miss Stokes. I'll have priceless modern talent on my walls and you'll be able to charge whatever you like!' He stood up as if to dismiss her. 'So, are you rushing off to your boyfriend now?'

She shook her head too quickly. It made her feel dizzy. The chair swivelled crazily of its own accord.

'It was just an innocent question.' He took the arms of the chair and spun it round to face him. 'I bet when you're scrubbed up you have them all eating out of your hand.'

'Scrubbed up?'

'Forgive me. Crass phrase. You're more like a pre-Raphaelite painting, that bone-structure, that Celtic colouring, your amazing hair, but why do you shroud it like this?' He waved his hand over her as if he was a conjuror. Her body went tight, watching his fingers as they cast their spell. 'I'm surprised that Sebastian hasn't seen the light, got you in front of the camera as well as behind it, because I'm sensing there's a sensational body under that dreary artist's smock or whatever it is you're wearing, just waiting to bust out.'

'You speak to all your employees like that?' she retorted weakly, even as the thought occurred to her that Cedric might be right. Jake wanted to hide her away. Keep her to himself.

This time Cedric Epsom's laugh was deep and dirty. He bent closer. Late evening silvery bristles were pushing through his tanned skin and he smelt divine. Sharp, crisp, lemony. She tried to suppress a sudden, vivid image of him patting the cologne on to his skin this morning in some vast marble bathroom, his face and naked body reflected in a huge, spotlit mirror.

'You're freelance, yes? So you're not exactly my employee. But yeah, if people don't like the way I say it, they don't have to take my money.'

She flinched like a ticked-off schoolgirl. She could picture Jake shaking his head at her uppity little gaffe. *Knew you couldn't cope out there without me.*

'Seriously, how do you think I'm so successful?' Cedric Epsom went on, hitching one buttock onto his desk. 'Once I've sussed the intellectual talent in a person, I can detect their physical potential under the thickest specs, the baggiest clothes, the drabbest of barnets. Get rid of that and you've got a force of nature who can do anything.'

Eloise stole another glance at his exquisitely cut trousers, the slight gather beneath the belt, but was that a bulge straining at the cloth, a long shape extending to the left of the zipper? Her stomach contracted and she flattened one hand against the plate glass window.

'I spotted that potential as you call it, just by walking through your lobby just now. Everyone who works here seems to be beautiful.'

He studied her. 'By the time we're through, you'll be beautiful, too, Miss Stokes.'

'I can't wait.' Eloise tried a little sarcasm. Show Cedric. Show Jake, that she could do this. 'So, tell me what you want from me.'

'God, Eloisa. Have you any idea how sexy that sounds?' His voice was gravelly now and he turned to the window. A descending aeroplane cut a swathe through the peachy evening sky. 'There's all sorts of things I want from you.'

'I meant, exactly what do you want from this commission?' It was supposed to sound curt, but was virtually a whisper. She watched the pulse go in his neck. 'How did this conversation get so suggestive?'

'Of course. Sorry. You're just so – there's something so raw about you.' There was a pause as he tried to hide the definite warp in his deep voice. 'Right. I want you to get under the skin of my family. Observe them. Position them. Frame them. Turn what you see into an amazing artistic moment.'

Surely that wasn't a catch in his voice?

'I think I understand.'

'A permanent memory, on celluloid, of one night before we all separate.'

There was suddenly something very still about him. All that ferocious power and energy temporarily contained as his words hung in the air. They both turned to each other at the same time, and suddenly her face was trapped between his big strong hands. She stood up on tiptoe but still she was only on a level with his throat.

'What are you doing to me, Miss Stokes?' Cedric reached out and twined his fingers in her wild, curly auburn hair, making her scalp tingle.

'I think the question is, what are you going to do to me?' she whispered, hardly believing she'd said it.

He smiled, something of the wolf returning to his grin. What big teeth you have. All the better for … He stroked her hair as if she was a nervous animal that needed calming. How was he to know how much she loved having her hair stroked? Even if he might be about to gobble her up?

'I'll come clean and confess. I asked you to come here because I wanted you.'

'Oh, God. You were reading my mind!'

He pulled her towards him. She could feel his breath on her face. She closed her eyes, taut with anticipation. Surely now he would dismiss her, finish the meeting before something disastrous happened, she hadn't meant that she wanted him, too, but it was too late, he started to kiss her, his mouth resting on hers, firm and masterful, his lips just hovering, and maybe he would have moved away then, but she gripped his shoulders, pressing herself against him, and that seemed to trigger all his responses and he wasn't going to stop now.

He nudged open her lips, running his tongue round the tender lining where all the little nerve endings burst into life, pulling away when she tried to suck at it, teasing her, making her want to scream, shout, kick, run away, tear her clothes off, but all the while his fingers tangling in her hair were hypnotic, keeping her very still.

She waited, still unsure of what to do, a very tiny voice in the back of her head questioning whether this was really the right way to close the deal.

But then he was kissing her again, and their bodies were pressed tightly together, heat radiating out of him. Sweat sprang up under her hair, the sky-high window cool against her back, the soft brush of her breasts such a contrast against his hard, muscular chest. All her senses were on high alert as he swayed her round in a strange dance, making her dizzy, her nipples hardening and grating against his cotton shirt, the friction kick-starting desire.

'This isn't right.' With superhuman effort she pulled away. 'Mr Epsom, I – I need to know that we still have an arrangement. That my behaviour won't spoil, won't change your view …?'

'That depends, Miss Stokes, on how good you are. Because I'm liking you more and more.' He laughed softly, more like a growl in his throat. 'And so will my family.'

Lust was sparking in his blue eyes now, a flush streaking his lean cheeks, and best of all, there was the unmistakeable response bulging out of the expensive fabric of his trousers, the way he shifted his weight towards her body, not away.

She pushed herself harder against him, her fanny damp inside her faded jeans as her body met the hard ready shape of his cock. Did his beautiful employees downstairs ever wonder, as they dawdled by the water cooler, if he was well hung? Come on. Had many of them tasted it?

Suddenly he fell back into the white chair, pulling her down on top of him. Distractingly, the lift bell outside his office dinged. Her head shot up at the distraction, and she could see against the darkening glass pane her face, wide-eyed, even wilder-haired, her breasts looking huge and dominant in the baggy shirt which oh God his long strong fingers were starting to unbutton.

Thank God Jake had bought her so much expensive underwear. He was absolutely right when he said a perfectly fitting bra and silky knickers would make her feel secretly sexy under all those scruffy clothes. And he said it made him feel horny knowing it.

He hadn't thought another man would be undressing her and enjoying his gifts, though, had he? But thoughts of poor Jake fled as Cedric Epsom opened the baggy blouse to reveal her big breasts squeezed into the frilly magenta bra. A muscle flickered in his cheek as that wolfish grin spread over his face again.

'La Perla. Who knew?'

As his mouth brushed against her breasts, swollen now and pulsing with excitement, she lifted one leg to straddle him, but then squealed with shock as he yanked her loose trousers and knickers right off.

Now his hands were squeezing her breasts so hard that they hurt, darkness sliding into light, pain into pleasure as he rubbed her nipples through the satin. Now her bare pussy was rubbing against his crotch, the length of his cock hard against her sex lips. She tried to let it rest there. If she moved he might stop, might even push her off, but she couldn't help it, she started writhing and grinding against the hard shape in his trousers until it nudged open her wet slit.

Her breasts were inviting white mounds in the twilight, twinned in the huge window. Across the way people still moved about in the offices, and she could see one or two heads bent over their desks by the window, close enough for her to call out to them.

Inside the Epsom Corporation power-house all she could hear was her own harsh breathing. With a low grunt Cedric Epsom scooped her breasts out of the bra and caressed them, flicking the berry-red nipples until they sang with excitement.

Her reaction was to jerk her hips, opening herself against the rigid shape of his cock still tucked inside his trouser. Cedric Epsom examined her breasts as if he was choosing a cream cake and she started to squirm with tipsy embarrassment. He deftly unclipped her bra and there they were, her breasts bouncing brazen and bare into his face.

Eloise rose up on her knees as if worshipping him, and gripped the back of the leather chair so they both rotated slightly and his face was forced between her breasts, his teeth nipping at one aching bud.

Eloise arched her back, desire crawling through her as he bit and sucked. She glanced at her naked reflection in the glass, and saw that in the office opposite, the heads that had been bent over their desks must have noticed what was happening, because several faces were staring across the void. Her stomach contracted with exhilaration. She opened her arms, inviting those strangers to stare as this man nibbled at her breasts, running her tongue over her lips as they strained to get a better look.

Now Cedric Epsom's cock was pushing against her and she scrabbled with his zip, her legs shaking with the effort of keeping upright.

As she opened his fly she stretched one foot to the floor and pushed the chair slightly so that it was sideways to the window. Now her voyeurs could see her taking out his cock, letting it stand upright on his stomach. She clamped her fingers round it, taking it prisoner, and aimed it at her cunt.

Her pussy was yearning towards it, knots of desire unravelling with urgency, her cunt twitching to welcome and swallow his cock, the damp curls of her bush tangled with moisture as she hovered over him. Cool guy that he was, he wasn't even breaking sweat as he bit at each stiff nipple.

Glancing again at her watchers who had jumped up from their desks and were unashamedly crowding round to see through the opposite window, Eloise started to sink on to Cedric, all the urges in her overpowering her.

'I can always tell,' he groaned, muffled by her soft flesh. 'A temptress under all that billowing cotton–'

That did it. She pushed herself at him so that the rounded end of his knob slipped just inside, setting fire to all her sensitive parts. She held his shoulders as she rocked very slightly, keeping herself upright so the others could see, letting his knob tease her burning clit, go no further inside, just tickling the surface, using him like her own toy before lowering herself slowly onto him. The smooth surface of his cock was already slippery where she'd slicked it with her honey, and the starting gun was about to go off.

She'd built up such a head of steam that she could come at any second if she wasn't careful, but she didn't want to make like an inexperienced virgin. One of the watchers across the way had binoculars, others were focussing their mobile phones, and she bit back a crazy giggle. She needed to keep them waiting, but she also desperately wanted to be fucked, have every last inch of Cedric Epsom buried inside her.

He stopped biting her and rested his head back on the chair, so cool, watching her like he was listening to someone at a conference, and she ground down hard, determined to make that impassive face lose control, no more messing, and as his cock made contact with the burning nub of her clit she moaned loudly. The pulsating length of him fitted hard inside her, a hot beast filling her, impaling her so that she could spin on it.

He tightened his grip on her hips as she slid right down to the base of his cock and they waited for the rhythm to begin.

The bell in the lift dinged again. Someone coming, or

going? Someone from inside, or out? Either way he didn't budge. Either way she wanted to scream with impatient delight. She thought she detected some kind of movement behind her in the window, but her reflection refused to co-operate or care, licking its lips like a harlot for the benefit of her watchers as she started to slide up and down his cock, making it grow harder and longer, every inch of him grazing every screaming inch of her so that she could only rise up so far before slamming back down on him.

'Hey, what's the rush?' He grabbed her hips to slow her down. He glanced at the workers watching them from the office opposite. He'd known all along. 'Got all the time in the world, haven't we?'

He looked relaxed in the chair but he wasn't slacking, far from it, because next thing he was ramming it up inside her as she thumped down to meet him and her moans rose to a crescendo.

Rivulets of fire streaked through her as her breasts bounced frantically, you couldn't miss them from halfway across the Thames, his calm eyes watching her as if she was a lap dancer and turning her on even more and then, as she curved and arched, failing to curb the inevitable, the climax breaking through her, his eyes glazed over, still trained on her as her body bucked and writhed over the top dog, on the top floor, watched by a crowd of horny City brokers, and his lips curled back into a splitting grin of pleasure and triumph as he threw her upwards with the force of his climax.

They were clapping! She could almost hear the distant round of applause as he let her rest for a moment on his chest, her legs aching from being spread so wide, then he let her fall sideways as he packed away his subsiding cock and stood up briskly.

Eloise slid back into the white leather chair, warm where he had been sitting, her leg hooked over the arm, swinging the chair round in circles, letting her audience see as she rubbed her aching pussy then sucked juices off her fingers, totally sated, totally debauched, totally amazed that she had pleasured this powerful guy, wondering if she was falling for him, wondering if he would come back for more

Wondering what Jake would say.

Chapter Three

THE INTERIOR OF THE enormous house in Richmond was all white, cream and blood-red, hopelessly elegant. Even the lilies in their tall vases were white, their stamens dusty red. Candles rested in faceted holders, waiting to be lit.

And against this pale background was a dark woman standing at the top of the stairs in a jet black diaphanous halter neck dress.

'You must be Eloise Stokes,' the woman purred, taking a step down the stairs. 'Welcome!'

She was silhouetted by the light from the huge arched window behind her like a pop star coming on to the stage. The setting sun provided a strong back light, shafting straight through the voile fabric of her dress and rendering it see-through. Mrs Epsom's incredibly slim thighs were slightly parted and flickering with impatient muscles as she rotated her foot in a black Laboutin sandal. As she lifted her leg to take a step down the stairs, the high-slit dress floated open at the top of her legs, briefly showing the corner, the curve, of one plump sex lip.

'Stop!' Eloise dropped her backdrop and lighting equipment on the floor in front of her and hoisted her favourite camera out of her bag.

'Why, honey, what's wrong?' Mrs Epsom halted as instructed, one knee cocked in front of the other, her slim arms reaching to each banister. Her face was in shadow, but as she adjusted the exposure Eloise could see her subject's large scarlet painted lips part slightly in surprise, showing perfect white teeth.

She was, just as Cedric Epsom had said, like a luscious Morticia Addams.

Eloise's finger felt slippery on the shutter. She'd made sure she was out of the gallery that day, and away from Jake and his questions, but that meant she had been sweating on location before coming here, desperate to see Cedric again. Thank God the heat was finally fading.

'Fuck. I'm sorry if that sounded rude – fuck, I shouldn't have said fuck – but Mrs Epsom, please could you hold it there, because I think I've got my Morticia Addams shot!'

Mrs Epsom laughed and shrugged one round, deeply tanned shoulder, looked over it, deep into Eloise's lens, twisted this way and that like a proper catwalk model. Then she continued her smooth descent.

'Darling, you're a little early, but that's not a problem. You can have me all to yourself. Just follow me round, and you can tell me where you want me.'

The house was all old world grandeur, but without the fuss. There seemed to be nobody else around. There was almost total silence other than the distant roar of the aeroplanes coming in and out of Heathrow and some classical piano music wafting faintly from speakers hidden near the corniced ceilings.

Getting into her stride, Eloise followed the woman from room to room, watching the way Mrs Epsom's buttocks twitched under the black voile as she walked ahead. The way her neat bottom caught the material between her butt cheeks, then softly released it again.

'So, Eloise, where do you want me?'

Eloise paced the huge wood panelled drawing room and opened the French windows to let in what was left of the natural light.

'Here. I'd like to try something fairly formal, classic, you know? Just your face and shoulders, Mrs Epsom, looking out from these shadows into the garden.'

Mrs Epsom did as she was told and leaned dreamily in the doorway, resting her head on one upstretched arm. Eloise busied herself outside, setting up her tripod, making sure no direct sunlight fell on her subject. The light was perfect, and she started to shoot. Mrs Epsom kept her eyes focussed just past Eloise's ear as if she was staring out to sea, her red lips parted, her brown limbs totally still.

There was only the rise and fall of her breasts as she breathed, making the silk shiver over her skin. And the sweat trickling down Eloise's back.

Cedric Epsom appeared through another doorway, barking into a mobile phone.

'Christ, isn't my wife gorgeous, Miss Stokes?'

Eloise felt a blush suffusing her body at the sound of his deep voice. She kept the camera up in front of her face as Cedric flipped shut his phone and slipped his hand through the slit in his wife's dress where it fell open across her thigh.

'These Brazilian women are sex on a stick. Nothing like the chilly white Brits. You should feel how soft her skin is. How warm. Just up here, you know? Just where it meets and gets all damp, and divides into that lovely pussy.'

'You're embarrassing the poor girl, darling. She's shaking.'

'Just hold it like that.'

Eloise grew hotter and stickier but she jammed the camera against her nose to keep shooting. *Chilly white Brit.* Was that some kind of coded message for her to keep clear? Discarded plaything? As she watched them through her viewfinder Cedric's hand went right inside his wife's dress. Mrs Epsom's head fell back on his shoulder, her eyes fluttering closed, her lips parting wider. He wrinkled open the dress with his other hand, gathering the folds on her hip so as to expose her pussy. It wasn't even Brazilianed. It was totally waxed.

Eloise's own pussy felt like it was going to cook inside her denim shorts. She had deliberately chosen a prettier, gauzier top today, to please Cedric, make him admire her again with those laser eyes. It was loose and floaty, but it was already sticking to her armpits as she remembered Cedric Epsom's teeth biting her nipples the other day, his huge cock shafting her on that white leather chair, the City boys applauding.

But it wasn't going to happen again. She was a mere visitor, observer. Staff. He was the master of this house now, standing here proudly with his lovely wife, his hair slicked back, cool as ice in the dinner jacket yet stroking his wife's gleaming pussy, running one finger slowly up and down the red crack peeping between the lips, the inner fire blazing briefly pink as he tickled it open to show the camera, before it closed softly shut again. Bastard.

Mrs Epsom's tongue mirrored his finger, flickering over her mouth.

'I think we should leave it there? I can see you both want some privacy.' Eloise hurriedly backed outside.

'Why so coy, Miss Stokes? This is how we Epsoms always behave.' Cedric stepped out onto the terrace, leaving his wife to gather the family together. He grabbed Eloise's arm. 'Your work in the gallery was extremely horny. Not to mention our little *pas de deux* in my office the other day. You're a raging nympho under that mousy exterior, so don't pretend otherwise. That's why I hired you.'

'I think we should forget all about that. It was totally unprofessional. Of both of us.' Even though she still had a neat set of circular bruises to show for it.

'But going off-piste like that so smooths the path to good business relations, don't you think?' He folded his arms and chuckled, regarding her as if she was a sulky child. 'No need to get your wet little knickers in a twist just because I like to touch up my wife in front of you!'

Eloise took in a sharp breath. This was a job, remember. He was the client. 'My understanding was that this commission was for formal portraits. Not porn.'

'Well, I've found, now you're here, that touching her up in front of you and your camera is a turn on! Anyway, how can loving my beautiful wife be pornographic?' Cedric lowered his voice. 'But all right. I'll pay you double what we agreed if you succeed in capturing our more, ah, erotic moments.'

'So cute, isn't she, with those stern glasses and all that wild gypsy unbrushed hair.' Mrs Epsom floated in to the space between them and wound her arm round Eloise's waist. 'But I'd like to get my hands on you, sweetie. Straighten you out.'

Her dress was still open, the silk shifting across her thighs, catching in her pussy crack, attracted by the wetness there. She led Eloise back into the drawing room.

A girl and boy dressed like Goths were lounging on the sofa and another young man was leaning on the mantelpiece. The boys had Byronic long black hair, frock coats and foppish velvet bow ties. The girl was a delicate version of Wednesday Addams, wearing a tight black sheath dress which looked sprayed on to her. They were all so pale they were practically spectral.

As her shutter started to whir, Eloise relaxed and dismissed Cedric's outrageous suggestion as some kind of tease. This sitting was more like it. The family were perfect models. Not only did they have Alpine cheekbones that cast their own perfect shadows, they positioned themselves effortlessly in compositions with the luminous quality of a Singer Sargent painting, just as she intended. They were smiling or sombre to order, perfectly lit by the lowering sun and the gathering twilight, but it was still spookily like directing the Cullen family from the "Twilight" films.

As soon as the shot was in the can their faces froze into expressions more glowering and surly than any vampire.

The two boys were either very close in age or twins, she realised, and they were all, totally unlike the sultry mother, very pale skinned. When the session was over the daughter

93

ran up the stairs without a word and whipped off her black wig to let silky blonde hair ripple down her back.

Eloise smiled, just so pleased it was all over. 'Well, they are absolute naturals, Mrs Epsom, silent or not.'

'Call me Mimi, please. Now, will you stay for dinner? Cedric and I have another proposition for you.' She paused halfway up the stairs. 'Come with me, and I'll find you something more glamorous to wear.'

Eloise followed her heavy scent up the curving stone staircase and through some double doors at the end of the wide carpeted landing. This must be the Epsoms' bedroom. She felt a twist of jealousy at the thought of the two of them humping amongst the silk and velvet cushions, but actually there was not a single male object anywhere in the room. It wasn't a boudoir so much as an Aladdin's cave. Draped over the bed, over the chairs, on the shelves, was a multi-coloured array of sensational underwear and designer dresses.

Creamy satin knickers, midnight blue camisoles, burgundy bras with delicate straps, black basques, sheer pink stockings and see-through negligees, everything you could think of, were heaped in abundant piles around the room. A haughty mannequin posed in the window, dressed in a scarlet corset with suspenders and stockings to match, one plastic hand thrust brazenly between her legs and her chin tossed sideways.

'Oh, some of my underwear designs,' explained Mimi, trailing her hand through piles of lace. 'Now, Cedric has decided he wants more from this commission. Almost like a home movie. We want you to follow the family round, especially the kids. Get them *au naturel*. Intimate moments. A kind of montage.'

Up close Mimi had beautiful, velvety skin the colour of burnt toffee, and there was a light dusting of freckles over her throat, leading into the dark shadow between her breasts.

Eloise pondered. 'I don't have time, unfortunately.

They've all dispersed, and I thought they were all leaving home in a couple of days.'

Mimi sat Eloise on a low window seat and handed her a glass of champagne. 'That's why we want you to stay until Sunday morning. We'll be coming and going, and we want you to flit about like a little spook and capture all the chaos.'

'I could stay, yes, though I half expected Mr Epsom to ask me himself.' Eloise did a quick reckoning. The opportunity, the publicity, the fee, all too good to pass up for the sake of hurt pride. And it certainly wasn't worth telling Mimi about her rutting bastard of a husband.

'Oh, he acts the big man at work but I'm the boss around here, I assure you. He says he mentioned something to you earlier, when we were getting a bit frisky downstairs, but that you were embarrassed. So this extension of your commission was my idea. Give you a chance to get to know us.'

Eloise laughed nervously. 'OK. But forget I'm here. Like a shadow.'

'Not a chance. With a cute body like yours? This is the first time Cedric's allowed one of his beautiful protégées to cross the threshold.' Mimi dumped an armful of clothes on the seat. 'Consider yourself permitted to get in our faces, as the boys would say.'

As Eloise started to rifle through silky dresses and knickers Mimi lifted Eloise's thick hair and started pressing her fingers across the plates of her skull, massaging her scalp in a soothing motion.

'A makeover, I think,' she murmured, as if to herself. 'Shower first, then hair.'

Mimi led a drowsy Eloise across the soft carpet to the bathroom and started to run the water in the shower. Scented steam hissed out of the cubicle. Mimi unbuttoned Eloise's blouse before she knew what was happening.

Eloise felt even more shy than she had with Cedric, even when she was riding him like a bronco in front of a window full of watching strangers. But why? Was it the rapt attention Mimi was lavishing on her? Her exotic beauty? The dizzying scents and warmth of her bedroom? The fact that she was undressing her as if she owned her, singing under her breath as she unhooked the pale green bra Eloise was wearing to match the tunic?

'Everything off,' Mimi murmured, and Eloise obediently kicked off her tight denim shorts, her skin plumping out with relief at being free.

Mimi's eyes gleamed. Her hand went up to her throat and stroked the tender skin just above her breastbone.

'Oh my, what a treasure I've unwrapped! See how good you look naked,' she breathed huskily, stepping close and circling Eloise's waist with her hands. 'These long legs, I didn't notice those before. And these breasts, which I *did* notice. They could star in a portrait all of their own!'

Her dress was slipping elegantly off one smooth shoulder as she looked at Eloise with a witch-like intensity in her black eyes. Eloise blushed and stepped quickly into the shower and sprayed off the dust and sweat of a London day. She frothed the soap over her skin, buffing the blood so that her whole body tingled, holding her face under the needles of harsh spray until she was totally invigorated.

She turned the water off and groped about for a towel, and Mimi was there, rubbing her dry.

'I can't help it, Eloise.' Mimi rested her cheek against Eloise's face. 'You have no idea how cute you are.'

Eloise stood perfectly still, motionless with shock. Mimi took her silence for consent and kissed her cheek, moving her mouth slowly, her lips so warm and sweet that Eloise couldn't breathe.

Mimi pulled away and laughed softly. 'I just can't resist a challenge. If you haven't been touched by a woman before, I want to be the first one.'

Mimi's hands slid down Eloise's ribcage, over her hips, and round to her bottom, before stroking up again. Suddenly she whisked the towel away. They both gasped as Eloise's breasts thumped softly into Mimi's waiting hands, the nipples shrinking instantly into stiff points. A new ball of lust rolled in her stomach as Mimi moulded her breasts in her palms. She paused, then pressed them together, each forefinger circling each raspberry nipple.

Eloise couldn't look at her face. Her legs were shaking. To steady herself she went to grab Mimi's shoulder, but by accident, or not, her hand fell on the neck of Mimi's dress. It slithered away like a shy animal, falling off like a skin, and then one brown breast was exposed, round and ripe, with an incredibly large, chocolate coloured nipple sprouting in the middle. Mimi was casting her spell. The ball of lust in Eloise lurched, forbidden and intoxicating, seizing her with the violent, unthought-of urge to crush Mimi's swollen red mouth with hers, but even more perverted, to lick at that chocolate nipple, knowing it would harden with pleasure, knowing it would elongate and spring against her teeth.

Mimi guided Eloise back into the bedroom, where there was a huge, Venetian mirror dominating one wall. Eloise straightened, gazing at her pale, curvaceous, clean body prickling with all this untried pleasure. Mimi was smiling over her shoulder as her hands slid over Eloise's tingling breasts and away again. Eloise's green eyes, set wide apart, grew larger as she watched the brown fingers start to stroke down her stomach. Mimi's breath was so warm on Eloise's still-damp neck.

'Are you going to show me some dresses?' Eloise stammered into the silence.

'In a minute, sure. I'm going to transform you into a princess. But we can't have you going into battle without being warmed up, can I?'

'Battle?'

'You have no idea. Hanging out with that brood all weekend and coming up with award winning images. Cedric will expect nothing less, you know.'

Her idea of warming up meant walking her fingers down to Eloise's tawny bush, still curling and dark from the shower water. Her thighs parted eagerly, even though her legs were still shaking. Mimi's fingers paused, then tip-toed into the hidden crack, sliding down between lips until she reached the secret opening located there, then whisking up again.

Eloise stared at her reflection, her mouth gasping open. There was only one thing she wanted to do right now. Amazed at herself, she pulled Mimi roughly round so that they were breast to breast. Eloise pushed her still open mouth on to Mimi's. Her lips were like cushions, giving softly, letting Eloise try this out. She pushed harder, feeling a thrill at this tiny exercise in domination.

It felt so strange, making a move like this, like being a man. Yet Eloise had never felt more feminine.

Eloise flicked her tongue out and there was Mimi's, tickling the corner of Eloise's mouth. Eloise sucked it in against her teeth, and felt it probing, like a wee penis. Eloise nearly passed out with the shocking pleasure of it, made all the more intense as Mimi kissed her passionately, all the while stroking Eloise's pussy until it was vibrating with desire.

The two women started to writhe against each other, kissing greedily, their quiet female moans turning them on even more. Mimi pressed closer, her fingers probing up Eloise's cunt while her thumb relentlessly circled and teased Eloise's clit until sparks exploded in her head.

Eloise couldn't reach Mimi's pussy but grabbed her buttocks instead and spread them open. As her fingers slipped inside the warm crevice to explore this unknown place, she glanced sideways and saw the twin profile in the mirror, the pale body and the caramel coloured, hands roving greedily, her breasts and Mimi's breasts rubbing in sexy friction to keep their nipples rock hard.

Ecstasy started lapping at her, shafting out of Mimi's

fingers. Fingers and thumb playing her like a violin. Eloise wanted more than anything to do the same for this gorgeous woman, and she pushed her fingers urgently into Mimi's pussy, too, kissing her passionately, feeling the other woman's pussy sucking and tightening around her fingers, but it was suddenly too much, too soon. Waves of pleasure radiated like stars and Eloise moaned as the climax came, hot and quick.

They both sank to the carpet, still kissing but more gently now. Mimi's cunt was still twitching and moist, her long eyelashes fluttering against Eloise's cheek like butterflies.

'Wait for me, wait, we're not finished,' Eloise whispered into that luscious wet mouth as she pushed her fingers harder inside Mimi's cunt, instinctively knowing what to do and how rough to be. Mimi fell back onto the carpet and Eloise crouched over her, taking that chocolate nipple into her mouth and feeling it push against the roof of her mouth as she sucked it. Mimi bucked and arched with pleasure, pushing her breasts upwards as Eloise fucked her with her fingers until she moaned and screamed and came beneath her.

Above them, the mannequin's head had tilted to enjoy the view.

The numbers in the house had swelled as the evening wore on, and other guests had joined the party. Mimi led Eloise into the dining room. Her floaty virginal dress was a replica of Mimi's, only white. It was cut so low that her breasts wobbled precariously as if about to tumble out but were actually contained in cleverly constructed invisible cups, her nipples clearly visible against the delicate lace. The material fell away from her hips, revealing the pink cleft between her legs as she moved in the slow, sensuous way the dress invited.

They walked in, arms entwined, and the room fell quiet.

'Remember, princess,' Mimi whispered in her ear.

'Intimate moments.'

She sat down at one end of the table opposite Cedric, and a small man on the far side of the table pulled out the only other vacant chair for Eloise. Cedric ignored her, but all three of the youngsters, still wearing their gothic outfits and black wigs and dripping with jet jewellery, stared as if they'd never seen her before. What planet were they on? Yes, she was wearing a gorgeous dress and Mimi had brushed her hair into a burnished curtain, but was this really such a transformation? Was she really so dowdy and plain before?

Yes, she heard Jake mutter. *And that's the way I liked you.*

Across the table Mimi went into action. Her luscious red mouth pouted and smiled as she pinned a shy young man with glossy dark curls back in his chair with her charm. He was obviously a friend of one of the sons and looked like a prime stag caught in headlights.

A salmon mousse appeared, and Eloise fell upon it, suddenly ferociously hungry. And when she'd finished that, and two glasses of wine, she was also hungry for some attention. Neither Mimi nor Cedric caught her eye. The conversation was loud around the table, in various languages, and everyone started flirting and gesticulating exaggeratedly.

The man beside her talked pleasantly in a strong French accent about the perfume industry. Eloise laid her arm across the back of his chair, smiling sweetly as she relished the food, the wine, the candlelight, the wispy drape of the dress across her limbs. Not to mention the deep aching in her cunt from Mimi's fingers – and Cedric's cock just days before.

The attention came from her neighbour. He started to stroke her thigh, bare beneath the flimsy dress. He leaned in hungrily so that his nose was level with her just-covered nipples. One or two men started craning their necks to see what was happening up her end of the table. Eloise's neighbour lifted his glass to drink and tipped it sideways, spilling white wine right across her chest. She gasped out loud as the cold liquid trickled down between her breasts.

'*Excusez-moi!*' The little man flicked out his napkin and started dabbing painstakingly, snuffling his nose into her cleavage as he tried to dry her. The napkin tickled her skin, starting up little pin-pricks of pleasure in her nipples.

He saw her reaction, and still talking he allowed his other hand to claw the dress up her leg. Across the table she could see Mimi's hand stealing under the table and into the young man's lap. Eloise parted her legs. Her sapphic encounter with Mimi upstairs had made her hypersensitive to any touch, by anyone. She let the man push her dress right up, his stubby fingers to stumble into her warm bush, realised the entire table was staring at them now. She lifted one foot on to the arm of his chair so everyone could see even more. Her head swam with the idea of leading him on, getting pleasure, making his day, and being watched.

Across the table the cloth jerked up and down under the young man's plate as Mimi massaged his prick. He gaped helplessly, biting his lips to contain the yelp of lust threatening to burst out. Eloise's Frenchman scrabbled his fingers inside her even more frantically as their hostess masturbated her young guest. Everyone watched until there was one final thrust under the tablecloth.

The guy sank back in his chair just as Eloise's own gush of pleasure overcame her.

And across the table Mimi winked, licking drips of creamy dessert off her spoon.

Chapter Four

ELOISE COLLAPSED ON THE bed in her pretty guest bedroom with the amazing view from the balcony over the river. It was the early hours, and she was pissed, but she still had a job to do. She picked up her camera to scroll through the pictures she'd taken so far and edit any that didn't work.

She was pleased with the classical, almost comically stiff, compositions of the family portraits. The poses, the lighting, the setting, all was perfect. But then a couple more images flicked by. She was about to delete them because they seemed to be blurry and out of focus when she realised that they weren't hers. They were taken through a doorway, or window, and they were of two women, one pale and naked, the other dark and half dressed.

And reflected in the mirror behind them were the ecstatic faces of her, and Mimi, fingering each other earlier that evening.

She bit her lip, smiling to herself at the memory of that woman's hands, mouth, fingers. But she couldn't work out how the handful of images had got there. The only explanation was that she'd left the camera on self timer, except that she was certain she'd packed it carefully away. Either way, the pictures, out of focus as they were, were sexy enough to get her heart pounding again.

There was a knock at the door. She roused herself to answer and Rick, the older of the two sons, and his shy friend with the dark curls sauntered in.

'Hey, boys, it's very late,' Eloise murmured, holding the camera in front of her like a shield and crossing her legs.

'Everything all right?'

'Sure. I just wanted to introduce you to my mate from uni, Freddy,' drawled Rick, surprising her by tugging off his tumbling black curled wig and revealing the same silky blond hair as his sister. 'He's going to study photography next year and we thought you might give him some tips.'

Eloise sighed. 'I'd love to, but not tonight, eh? I'm exhausted.'

Rick smiled. He had a gorgeous wide grin and cheekbones like Nureyev. Freddy looked like a sheepish but hunky Mexican bandit.

'A night cap, then?'

Rick stood up and went to the cabinet in the corner of the guest room, and poured out three glasses of golden brandy. Eloise took one and kicked off her shoes.

'How was it for you down there at dinner, then, Fred?' Rick joked, as they lounged on the rug by the fire. 'Mimi's fingers wrapped round your cock?'

Eloise choked as the brandy went down the wrong way, but it broke the ice. Even the embarrassed Freddy laughed as she coughed and spluttered.

'I don't think we should be talking about her like that!' Eloise blushed furiously. She fiddled with the CD player on the table beside her. A cool, sexy sax silenced the boys' sniggering.

'But you think she's hot, too, don't you?' Rick topped up their glasses. 'I could see it your face when you both came in to dinner.'

'She's gorgeous, sure.' Eloise wriggled on her chair. 'But I'm not gay or anything.'

'Anyone with eyes and a pulse would fancy her. She's got a mouth like Angelina Jolie, tits like Jordan's but totally natural, and that forty a day voice,' persisted Rick. 'Come on, you only met Mimi this afternoon. How come you looked so, like, glued together when you came in to dinner?'

They were both staring at her. It felt pretty damn good,

two gorgeous young men at her feet. Eloise responded in the only way she knew how. By raising her camera. And it had the desired effect. The two boys instantly forgot the outrageous things they'd been saying and arranged themselves into dissolute poses, all pouting mouths, arrogant profiles, and lazy limbs. Though Freddy was undoubtedly the more masculine of the two with his square jaw and muscled arms, it was Rick she was contracted to photograph, and so Rick was the one she concentrated on.

'We shouldn't be talking about your mother like that,' she murmured finally, putting down the camera. Her head swam wonderfully as the brandy warmed her veins and the boys sat back, still staring at her. Particularly Fred, who had lust written all over his handsome features.

'Oh, Mimi's not my mother!' Both boys laughed even more. 'She's my new step-mother! That's why she was allowed to make free with my poor mate under the table. No one says no to Mimi Epsom. Dad's a stud at the best of times, but even she's running him ragged since they got married. She looks like she's permanently on heat!'

'That explains a lot.' Eloise walked unsteadily over to the fireplace and stared at herself in the huge mirror. 'All that newly wedded bliss.'

'But I didn't think she had a thing for women until this evening. So what went on between you and Mimi before supper? Did she come on to you in the bedroom when she was getting you all dressed up?'

'God, you're like a dog with a bone!' Freddy kicked Rick. 'Can't you see how red she's getting?'

'I'm a little tired, boys,' she murmured.

'You're the one with the bone, mate,' Rick persisted, running his hand over his crotch. 'You're the one who's had Mimi's little hand pumping on your cock.'

Freddy spluttered. 'Maybe she thinks you're off limits!'

'Well, I'm not. I've had the hots for her ever since Dad first brought her home, and I want to know what she's like.

What her hand felt like. What she's like in the sack. Give me a break, guys! Fantasising about her might be the only action I get tonight, for God's sake!'

Freddy guffawed unkindly, and Eloise giggled.

'She is very, very sexy, yes, and I don't think she'll stop until she gets what she wants.' Eloise spoke softly, pressing her cheeks between her hands as she went and sat in the low armchair by the fire. 'She rubbed me dry after I came out of the shower, and then she kissed me. My first kiss with a woman.'

'Oh God, I bet that was divine.' Rick knelt up and put his hands on the arms of the chair. 'Show me what she did.'

Eloise bit her lip, then ran her lips across Rick's mouth. She could feel how smooth and boyish his skin was, but also the rough bristles coming up on his chin. His mouth opened slightly, and she tickled her tongue across his bottom lip, warming with pleasure when she felt the lust shudder through him.

'You bastard, Rick,' breathed Freddy, watching them. 'You know I fancied Eloise!'

'Guys, guys, cool it. I'm not some kind of trinket!' Eloise pushed Rick away from her. 'You're both – well, pick on someone your own age.'

'You're only a couple of years older than me. Mimi's ancient,' Freddy muttered. 'But Rick still wants her.'

'Shut it, Freddy. She's Dad's trophy wife. Thirty-five, tops. So, tell us more about her, Eloise. What happened next?' Rick elbowed his friend so that he fell back on the floor.

'You're not going to give this up, are you?' Eloise sighed. 'Well, she pulled the towel off, so I was naked.' They waited, mouths hanging open. 'We stood in front of the mirror, so we could see what was going on. And then she touched me. On my stomach.' Eloise touched herself there. 'My breasts.' She fanned out her fingers and cupped her almost bare breasts over the flimsy lace. They were bouncing with her heartbeat. 'And my pussy.' She paused, teasing them, teasing herself, refusing to move her hands further down even though their little tongues were hanging out now. 'She touched me everywhere. And then we kissed again.'

'Oh God,' both boys growled in unison. 'Show us again, Eloise. Please show us!'

Eloise hesitated, then stood up shakily and stepped over them to stand in front of the fire. She looked down at their flushed faces, the huge bulges in their trousers, the bubbles of saliva gathering at the corner of their moist young mouths, and she felt the wetness springing between her legs.

She started to push the white dress off her shoulder, relishing the whisper of it across her skin. She pulled it down to where her breasts were encased in the lacy cups, aware that her heavy breathing was making her breasts rise and fall. They were swelling out of the dress.

The boys were both staring, making the nipples harden and prick against the lace. She unfastened the one hook that held the dress across her body, cocking her leg so that the dress fell open across her thigh, held it closed for a moment longer as she stood above them.

Then she wriggled a little, freed her breasts from the lacy cups. They fell heavily forward, and the dress slithered right down to the thick carpet where the boys were lying.

'You were totally naked?' breathed Rick, his hand massaging his crotch now.

'Oh, man,' Freddy just groaned, muscles flickering in his cheek as he willed his erection not to show.

'Yes, we were both naked,' Eloise answered quietly, catching sight of her reflection in the mirror. 'Two women, one dark, one pale.'

Her breasts were jutting forward from her slim frame, wobbling with her rapid heartbeat, full and swollen with excitement caused by her words and the boys' burgeoning admiration.

She started to stroke and knead them, gently at first, then more firmly. Rick and Freddy swore under their breath as her own little floor show began. The two beautiful boys watching her, bodies rigid with expectation, was rousing her to fever pitch. They were going to watch, and then she was going to make them fight over her. She didn't care which one of them fucked her, but she knew that she wanted a young, hard cock plunging in to her very, very soon.

'Did she make you come, Eloise?' Freddy asked. He sounded as if he was far away, and his voice had descended several octaves. 'Did she make you come with her fingers? Is that what women do to each other?'

Rick gave a low chuckle at his friend's daring. Or perhaps he was shocked that his friend was joining in.

'Yes, now I know what women do to each other, because I had my fingers inside her, and I made her come, too,' Eloise answered, flicking at her nipples with her thumbs and letting out a moan of her own. 'And, oh, I'm ready to come again.'

'Please, Eloise, let me. I think you're so gorgeous–' offered Freddy, undoing the collar of his shirt and running his hand through his curls, now getting wet with sweat. 'I'm going to explode if I don't do something with this!'

A great surge of hot lust pounded through her as the boys wound each other up, daring each other, all the time watching her. The jazzy music wound around as she caressed her breasts more passionately, swaying and letting her hair swing down her back. The touch of it on her skin reminded her of Mimi, stroking her hair, transforming the ugly duckling, as she had called it. If only Mimi could see her now.

'You're getting hard watching me, aren't you, boys?' The heat curled up from her cunt. What would Mimi do?

'Christ!' spluttered Freddy, falling dramatically backwards on the carpet. 'This is like the best wet dream!'

The sight of the beautiful dark boy lying back on the

107

carpet, his blond friend unzipping his flies to get at his swollen cock, was too much for her. Eloise put her knees on either side of Freddy and straddled him.

'Oh, fuck, oh fuck!' Freddy lost the power of speech. He reached up and grabbed at her breasts, pushed them together and started to suck her nipples like an eager puppy. She hissed with pleasure and arched her back into him, which meant that her butt was sticking up in the air.

She could easily have come, just from his sucking her nipples, but she wanted something more. She crawled further up until her crotch was in his face. His hands stroked up the back of her legs. She pushed her velvety pussy lips aggressively against his face and felt his breath blow across the bare skin. She started to sway her hips, desire pulsating through her.

'I think I'm in love,' mumbled Freddy, grasping her buttocks, pulling her pussy against his mouth. Behind her, Rick sniggered and swore again. Freddy's tongue touched her clitoris and she let out a loud moan, grinding herself harder against Freddy's face.

Rick was on all fours, snarling like a dog behind her. He pulled her roughly off Freddy, so that she fell spread-eagled on the carpet, arms and legs spread in what could only be interpreted as a welcome.

And sure enough they were both all over her like climbing ivy, stroking and kissing her prone body, pulling her legs open. One of them held her hands and lashed her wrists with a tie. She rolled and twisted as they manhandled her, always biting and licking, one of them coming up the inside of her thighs with his mouth, the other kissing round her neck, pulling her hair out of the way, biting hard like the vampires they were, then heaving up her breasts so that her taut nipples were offered upwards. She wriggled and squealed, imagining herself floating above the scene, the camera clicking away of its own accord, recording the fantasy.

She didn't think she could hold out much longer. 'Take me, someone, for God's sake fuck me!'

Rick was on it. 'I'm going first. Don't mind do you, mate?'

'I'll watch. It'll be almost as good. She's so gorgeous.' Freddy sounded as if he was in some kind of trance. She glanced sideways, saw him sitting back on his haunches, those dark curls tight with sweat, his dark eyes gazing at her like a love-sick spaniel. Something inside her melted.

She stretched her hand out. 'Hey, Freddy. It'll be worth waiting for, I promise.'She kept her eyes on Freddy as Rick lay down on top of her, breathing heavily, his blue eyes glazed just like his father's. He kissed her hungrily, then pushed her legs further apart. Freddy would be getting an eyeful. Then Rick eased his throbbing dick up inside. Eloise got a dirty kick out of how debauched this all was, how they were all tasting something new, and suddenly Jake's face flashed across her mind. But instead of looking angry, or hurt, he was bright eyed with excitement, nodding his approval.

Rick thrust his big cock inside her and she gave in to it, her breasts bare and swollen, her mouth wide with ecstasy.

'She's wet, see, and welcoming. There won't be anything left for you,' Rick gloated, and Eloise steeled herself to keep her release for the love-sick Freddy.

She wrapped her legs round his waist as Rick started to thrust himself in. She was determined to keep herself back, stifling the urge to let the waves of her climax break, especially when Rick thrust harder and harder to reach his goal, his bollocks slapping against her as he gave in, biting her neck as he came.

Her body already ached and felt deliciously bruised. She was light-headed and confused, barely aware of how long she had been aching like this, who was here, who was inside her, who was watching.

Now Freddy was pulling Rick off. Rick swore and swung

round as if to punch Freddy, but Freddy was too fast. They started play fighting on the floor like that scene from *Women In Love,* their shirts hanging open, their cocks bouncing furiously in the firelight, like lions fighting for the pride, and Eloise lay back and smiled at it all.

And then Freddy was on top of her, and he darted his head down and caught one nipple in his mouth, biting it hard again, sending sharp messages of desire through her. She trembled with the mingled pain and pleasure. Keeping his teeth round the burning bud, he raised her buttocks towards his groin, bending his head so that he could still bite her breasts and at the same time aim the tip of his cock towards her cunt.

'Just fuck me, Freddy,' Eloise groaned, digging her fingers into his young flesh.

His cock was huge. Larger than Rick's. Larger than Cedric Epsom's. And, disloyal as it sounded, much larger and thicker than Jake's. She squealed with delight. It seemed to go on growing as it slid inside her, pulling out again to tease her, then thrusting in a little more, teasing, probing, nudging in and around her aching pussy, testing, tasting, exploring. Oh boy. He'd done this before.

'Let's see if we can make this last, really piss him off,' he panted into her ear. God, he was sexy. Her breath was jagged now. Freddy arched his back, thrust the length of his incredible cock into her, and speeded up the jerking of his buttocks.

Her arms were tied above her head, but she could still squeeze him tight with her thighs as they started pounding together, the ecstasy gathering into an exquisite point, ready to explode, the cool, sardonic Rick watching all the while, maybe taking pictures with her camera, who cared, her whole body convulsed and Freddy was coming too, his cock pumping, her body gripping him like a tight glove, squeezing every drop of pleasure out of him until the pleasure rippled, burst, and faded.

110

'Let me go, Freddy,' she whispered shakily, rolling over and feeling the sticky fluid slicking across her thighs. 'The night's still young. There's plenty more where that came from. But we can't do it if I'm all trussed up.'

'Oh, you look fine just the way you are,' taunted Rick, standing up as Freddy unravelled the bow tie from her wrists. 'But sadly, I have a plane to catch.'

As the door closed behind him, Eloise and Freddy looked at each other, slow smiles spreading over their faces as they reached out to take some more.

Chapter Five

SOMEONE HAD OPENED THE window. From the bed Eloise could see the river sparkling through the ornate railings of the balcony. The sun was already lying in a heavy square on the floor, where her dress lay limply like a discarded scarf.

Freddy had gone. She dashed out of bed, looked in the bathroom, stepped out on to the balcony. There was no sign of him. Only the bites on her neck from the vampirical Rick, and the fading rash on her chin from Freddy's all-night, passionate kisses.

Her heart sank with disappointment. She had really liked him. His naked adoration. His deep voice. His enormous cock. And she thought he'd fallen for her. But in the bright light of another hot day it all seemed like a psychedelic dream.

She opened her bedroom door, called out, but there was total silence. She picked up her camera and wandered on to the balcony. She was about to flick through last night's images when she saw what looked like the tip of an arrow slicing across the surface of the river. The arrow elongated into the prow of a narrow boat, skimming across the surface of the water, and now she could see stretching forwards, as if reaching for something, a pair of muscled arms pulling on a pair of oars. Then the rower leaned back, almost lying flat, the blades lying across his groin as he pulled, his big thighs tightening as his knees took the strain.

He must have noticed her moving on the balcony, because he glanced up, and no wonder. She was standing there in the bright sunlight, totally naked, with her russet hair flowing round her shoulders. No point hoping he wouldn't know who she was, because although he had his blond hair in a pony tail and was wearing a white vest this morning, which clung to every ridge of his spine and ribs, she knew damn well who the young sculler was. It was Jake. And behind the requisite shades he was getting a good look at her as he flew past.

Well, too late now. Butt naked or not, she couldn't miss this opportunity. She picked up her camera and zoomed in on him, capturing action shots when he was bent forwards, eyes forward, then pulling back, gliding fast with the oars crossed in front of him almost delicately, making neat puddles in the water, the droplets flying up round him like diamonds tossed into the sun.

And then he was gone. All that brawn and beauty packed into a fine young body, sweating and straining to power through the water.

She sat down at the little table, the sun hot on her shoulders. It must be nearly midday, but it was dawn before she'd gone to sleep. She shivered with remembered pleasure and glanced through her pictures. Half afraid, half hoping that she'd imagined the mysterious out of focus shots of her and Mimi. But sure enough, there they were, the hazy women in Mimi's bedroom last night, and their even hazier reflections in the Venetian mirror.

But there also was a handful of new ones; fragments of naked, young, straining bodies. Out of focus shots of her on all fours closing right in as Freddy's tongue lapped at her pussy. Rick pulling her off, taking his turn with her. Another glorious one of Freddy straining above her, his magnificent dark cock standing proud of his body, about to push inside.

She sat back in her chair, heart pounding all over again, and stared out at the empty stretch of river. A spindly footbridge linked the garden with a little island out there, and the scene was beckoning her with watery fingers.

She ran downstairs, ravenously hungry now. The house

was spookily silent, but in the enormous kitchen, coffee (mysteriously hot), orange juice and croissants were laid out on the breakfast bar. After she'd polished everything off she found a note: *Rick gone to Oz, Cedric at meetings, Honey and Mimi out shopping – So Jake is your subject for today.*

She grabbed some mineral water from the Smeg fridge and ten minutes later she was running across the footbridge in her underwear, a towel and camera bag flying up behind her, dropping everything on to the ground, and diving into the cold water.

The beach on the far side of the little island was deserted. There were some trees shielding her from the unblinking windows of the riverside mansions, one or two boats chugging or gliding through the river. But otherwise she was alone.

The sun was beautifully warm after the bracing water. Aeroplanes slid lazily over London, sun flashing off their metal bellies.

She flopped down on to the big white towel, her heart still drumming, body still buzzing. She stretched her legs out, pointed her toes. Glanced around. Slipped off her sopping wet bra and knickers.

A breath of air tickled her slightly parted fanny. She opened her legs a little more. Her hand flopped onto her bare stomach, fingertips moving down to the hairless groove along the top of her thigh. The surface of her skin was more sensitive for being in the open air. So sensitive she could come with a butterfly kiss. Her hand wandered back up towards her breasts, brushing across them, enough to make them swell hopefully, enough to make her stomach flutter expectantly.

The sun pressed on her eyelids as her hand traced circles and her nipples puckered up. Her thighs fidgeted on the towel, opening further. Her fingers caught at a hardening nipple. The other hand sidled into the warm tangle of hair over her pussy, pulling one or two strands upwards, the roots tugging on the tender skin. Her middle finger stroked the crack. The lips were wet, and not from the river. She wiggled her finger at the sliver of sensitive flesh, teasing it into tingling response. She moaned, turned on by her own voice, sure that she was alone.

And then a shadow crossed her face. She shifted, thinking a cloud was obscuring the sun. She shaded her eyes and saw a figure standing a couple of feet away. She raised herself on her elbow, her breast swinging heavily against her arm. A droplet of juice trickled across her thigh.

It was Jake, god-like in his vest and Lycra shorts. His body was honed from all that training, manly and muscular, but his face was still boyish. He was a younger, more innocent version of his steely older brother. Hectic flushes of blood were visible under his smooth skin. His bright blue eyes were fixed unashamedly on her big breasts. Well, they were bare and hanging there boldly in the sunshine. Where could a boy look? Her nipples hardened again into little arrows, pointing straight at him.

Jake swallowed and scuffled his bare feet in the dust, trying to adopt a kind of swaggering stance. Through his tight shorts his groin was bulging.

'They've all buggered off for the day. Said I had to make myself available.'

'You did great. I got some tremendous shots of you on the water just now.' Her voice pierced the humming silence. 'You rowing at Henley this summer?'

'Yeah, and tomorrow I'm going with my crew to a training camp in the States.' He glanced back at his boat, pulled up on the little shore behind him. 'Best way to work off a hangover. Everyone went a bit crazy last night.'

The fluttering in Eloise's stomach was back with a vengeance. It was twisting and tightening with lust. She wondered if Rick had given him the low-down on what went on in her bedroom, and embarrassment flooded through her. She wriggled the towel from under her and draped it over herself.

'Want some water?'

'My dad says you should never accept drinks from strangers,' he croaked with a lopsided grin, squatting down beside her and taking a swig.

'Oh, I'm totally harmless! I only attack people with my camera.' She waved the bottle at him. 'But I'd say you're big enough to take care of yourself.'

She patted the towel beside her. Big was the word. Oh yes. That hard-on was threatening to bust his pants.

She quietly took the bottle from him, keeping her green eyes calmly on his burning blue ones. Without wiping the neck of the bottle she flicked her tongue round the wet rim before taking a deep swallow. Now his eyes were on her throat as the cold liquid swished down.

'Did my brother bother you last night?' he asked suddenly. 'I saw him and Freddy going into your room.'

The bottle hovered above her open mouth as she pondered her reply.

'Some pretext about Freddy studying photography.'

'He is, actually. Here in London.'

Interest flickered inside her for another day. 'Whatever. What they really wanted was to ask me what I got up to with Mimi.' She licked the bottle again with a suggestive wipe of her tongue. 'Did you know Rick fancies your stepmother?'

He blushed even harder. 'Yeah. I've told him he's a perv.'

'Not really a perv. She's one sexy lady, after all.' A wicked thought occurred to her. 'Do you want to see some photos of what we got up to?'

Without waiting for his answer Eloise handed him the camera, starting with the out of focus pictures she'd found of the three of them fucking last night. This was probably way out of order. But then all the lines had become blurred since Cedric walked into her life.

As Jake scrolled through the pictures, biting his lip with

obvious lust, she leaned back, resting the bottle between her legs. She resisted the urge to run it up and down her hot slit like a sex toy.

'Fuck. These are sensational. Pure porn!' His young voice dipped violently into a deeper manly timbre, at odds with his adolescent face. 'Just wait till I speak to Rick. The three of you at it! Dad didn't tell us you were – Christ this is hot!'

Eloise's cunt gave a couple of uncontrollably cheeky twitches as she saw the effect the pictures were having on him. On his cock. The bottle slipped between her sex lips and nudged the tiny bud of her clit. She gripped it with her legs, droplets of condensation mingling with her own sweat and moisture.

'But who took them?' Jake took one last lingering look at the pictures, then switched off the camera.

She shrugged, and the towel fell off. Her breasts thrust out and Jake stared at the instant tightening of her red nipples.

'It's a total mystery,' she murmured, trying to act very calm, sit very still so as not to alarm him. 'Looks like a voyeur got into the house. Either that, or one of the family. One of the staff. Who knows? There are others of me and Mimi, too. Would you like to see them?'

'Oh, God. Yeah.'

Like an animal tempted in from the wild, he shifted a bit nearer to her, rubbing his blond hair off his hot face. They looked at the fuzzy images, both breathing heavily now.

'Or how about trying the real thing?'

He was giving in. She loved him for trying so hard to hold back, not be rampant and arrogant like his brother, but even though he was trying to make conversation he couldn't keep his eyes off her nipples, growing darker and harder and impossible to ignore.

The softest of breezes caressed her bare skin.

'I can't,' he croaked after a moment. 'I've never done it –

not properly–'

Oh, that was all the encouragement she needed. A gorgeous sweet boy, just legal, and ripe for deflowering. It was her turn to be the older woman.

Eloise tilted forwards on to her knees, pausing as he ogled her tits bouncing right there in front of him as if they were ice creams on offer. Softly, softly, catchee monkee ...

She picked up one large hand which was digging frantically about in the sand. She lifted it like a warm animal and placed it on one swollen breast. Her nipple spiked against his palm. His fingers sank into the soft flesh, making it ache with wanting. She spread her knees a little to balance more comfortably, dislodging the bottle. She leaned back so that her spine was arched and her breasts pushed at him, jumping up with each heartbeat.

The dry grass rustled in the slight breeze, and the waves curled on to the shore with a collective sigh, awakened by the wake of a passing boat. Her breasts disappeared between his hands. His blue eyes blazed with a helpless request for permission. They were both panting openly now.

Her head was limp and heavy on her neck. The only energy was fizzing between her legs. She was ready to sink beneath him, open arms and legs, let him grab and take and thrust and pummel. She wanted to make him into a man. Privacy, heat, open air, a boy with the body of a god. And all the time in the world.

She watched his fingers exploring the feel of her breasts, wandering across them and moulding them, pushing them together, letting them fall, playing with them, staring at the rigid raspberry nipples. Then she knelt and pushed them into his eager face. There was an electrifying pause. His breath whistled. She wanted him to nuzzle in, lick, suck, bite. His first real woman. Forget any teenage gropings he might have enjoyed. She wanted this to be what he'd tell his mates, tell his brother, remember forever. His first time.

He buried his face between her breasts. She rubbed one

taut dark nipple across his mouth. The tip of his tongue flicked out tentatively. Her knees wobbled and she clutched his shoulders. Her tit angled itself right into his mouth.

Again his tongue flicked out. Hands that a few minutes ago had been pulling on those oars were crushing her breasts, making them sing with pain. Then his soft lips took the nipple, drew the burning bud into his mouth and sucked. She cradled his blond head, his fierce sucking making her whole body ripple with desire.

She glanced over the quiet river, the heat shimmering round the big empty house, a bird hopping close to them on the dust, this beautiful boy sucking at her aching nipple. He took the other breast, turning from one to the other, lapping and sucking, groaning, biting and kneading harder, and her body was starting to give way. His mouth was rougher as he got the hang of it, so she pushed harder against him, daring him, searching for more pain to communicate more pleasure.

She parted her legs and straddled him, slowly pushing him over so that, still sucking on her, he fell on his back. Now her tits were dangling over him, their size and weight accentuated by hanging there, the soft globes pale in his brown fingers. She tilted her pussy desperately towards his groin and rubbed it against his shorts, the material rubbing against her skin, his dick hard and ready.

Still pushing her tits in his face, she grabbed at the shorts and started to roll them off him like a second skin. He raised his hips obligingly. His erect cock thumped free, juddering out from the rough tangle of blond curls, pulsating and ready. God, it was a work of art as cocks always are. She must do a photographic study. Its surface smooth like velvet, the mauve plum emerging from the soft foreskin, already gleaming.

She grabbed her camera, and took some pictures of it, outlined like a monument by the dazzling sun. Then she tossed the camera aside and folded her fingers round it. Time to try something new.

119

'You ready for this, Jakie?'

He didn't reply, just fell back as she slithered towards his groin. She reached his dick, standing up like a beacon. The tip already beading in anticipation. She'd never done this before, but it looked so tasty.

She drew his cock into her mouth, using her teeth as well as her tongue, relishing his groans of shocked pleasure as his knob knocked at the back of her throat.

His buttocks clenched as she sucked the sweet length of him. He started to buck, groaning in amazement. Eloise wondered if any of his pert little girlfriends gave head like this. Judging by his response, she doubted it. But she'd started now, and she wanted him to think he'd died and gone to heaven. Any minute now she was going to heaven, too. She was just preparing the way.

As she sucked, she rubbed her tits and pussy up and down his stretched-out legs. He pulled at her hair. She must slow herself down. She didn't want to waste this golden moment by letting herself come all over his shin bone. Her pussy was clenching frantically now, leaving slicks of juice all over his legs.

She gave it one last, long suck, then let it slide out, along her tongue, through her nipping teeth. Greedily she clambered back on top of him, tilting herself over him. 'See how beautiful it is,' she crooned, showing him the length of his glistening shaft encircled by her fingers. 'See how well it's going to fit.'

She aimed the tip of his cock towards her soft bush. She let it rest there, just nudging it into the landing strip of curls, watching the struggle in his face between letting her take charge, worrying that he might come too quickly, adding to the mix the danger of discovery, but there was no turning back now. She gasped as each inch went in, reaching under him to cup his balls and see him bite his lip with more loud groans of surprise.

This tension was ecstasy, but she couldn't hold on for

much longer. Slowly, luxuriously, the boy's knob slid up inside, all the way to the hilt. So tempting to ram it, let their hips start working, but she forced herself to pull away again. He frowned, but she was playing with him, easing herself down down again, moaning and tossing her head, and the next time he was with her, learning fast, pulling his own hips back, watching her all the time, then something across the river caught his eye and he froze.

'They're back!' he hissed, jamming his hands on her hips to hold her still.

'Who?'

'The others. I can see Mimi in the garden.'

'Then we'd better hurry up!' Eloise hissed back.

A filthy grin spread across his face, and suddenly he was looking at her in a different way. Almost domineering.

'Or someone will be taking more pictures?' he murmured.

She laughed as he pulled her forwards, jamming her tits into his mouth again and as first one nipple then the other ground into his mouth the rhythm started again, her body tightening to keep him inside her, his cock hardening with each thrust.

There was definitely movement over at the house. Mimi was on the lawn, shading her eyes, trying to see over to the island. Honey was on the balcony outside Eloise's room. Was that glass glinting in her hands? Binoculars, or a telescope? Eloise didn't care. In fact, she felt quite exhilarated at the thought of being watched as she did it *alfresco* with the princeling of the house.

Thank God the camera was with her, though. She didn't want anyone snooping through her pictures, least of all her influential employers – at least not until she'd completed this contract and got her money.

And that did it. The thought of those grainy images, someone watching and taking pictures of her with Mimi, kissing and touching in front of the mirror, her with those

121

two boys in her room last night, Rick and his insolent sexiness, eager, infatuated Freddy and his amazing cock, young Jake jerking and thrusting under her now, ramming into her, his hips drumming on the ground faster and faster, rutting rapidly until they both came and he shouted out loud, his voice echoing across the water, scaring a trio of ducks to flap awkwardly into the air.

Chapter Six

ELOISE WATCHED THE RED tail lights of the Range Rover disappear round the bend in the gravel drive. It was weird standing on the doorstep, waving them off like she was the lady of the manor, but they'd told her to make free with the house and all its contents while they were out.

Earlier they'd had drinks and a barbecue on the lawn with some respectable neighbours as a hazy twilight dropped like a veil over London. Eloise had kept her distance, padding about in the background taking "happy family" shots of Cedric tossing sausages and Jake moodily mixing Pimm's and trying to catch her eye. Mimi standing on the jetty blowing cigarette smoke into the darkness and Honey, barely touching a lettuce leaf, lying on the swing-seat and tapping endlessly on her iPhone.

Just after midnight Cedric and Mimi piled Jake's bags into the car to drive him to Heathrow. Jake hesitated beside Eloise.

'Call me. Please? I'll never forget today,' he whispered, pushing his mobile number into her pocket as he kissed her cheek. 'And when I get back from New York, I want to do it again.'

'So try it out on the American cuties first. See how they like it!' she whispered back.

Little did he know that Freddy's number was tucked in there, too ...

'And then there were two.'

There was no answer as Eloise turned wearily into the house. Much as she longed to go to sleep, or better still, go home to her attic flat in Earl's Court she still, as Cedric had rather curtly reminded her, had one part of her commission to complete.

She glanced down to check through her most recent shots, and when the camera whirred into life, illuminating each frame, she stumbled back against the wall with shock, making a vase on the table rattle.

Because loaded onto the camera were yet more fuzzy pictures, taken as if with a long zoom lens across the river towards the little island. They showed her emerging from the water after her swim, lying back on the sand in her soaked underwear and touching herself. Jake sneaking up from his boat and watching her, his shorts bulging with excitement, and then the two of them *in flagrante* as she deliciously deflowered him, sucking his young cock, her breasts dangling down over his eager lapping mouth.

They were beautiful shots, subtle and dreamy, but they were also dead sexy. Her cunt twitched. But also she was getting really spooked now. Who was watching her? Who was taking these pictures?

The sound of glass rattling from the kitchen distracted her, and she hurried to investigate. All the barbeque paraphernalia had been cleared away by the maids and the place was spotless, except that the fridge door had been left open. Bright light spilled out onto the pale tiled floor.

She was about to go and shut it but there, sitting cross legged in front of the fridge, her face lit with an eerie blue hue, was Honey. Her golden hair was tied up in a loose bun on top of her head, and she was spooning left-over trifle into her mouth direct from the crystal bowl, and then washing it down with a big bottle of lemonade.

Eloise raised her camera and clicked. Honey looked like Kim Basinger in the famous scene in *Nine And A Half Weeks,* right down to the luscious mouth and the sexy greediness with which she was stuffing pudding into her mouth, licking her lips, then picking strawberries out of a punnet and swallowing them whole.

'Hey, that looks good. Can I have some?'

Honey glared at her, chewing silently as Eloise sat down beside her. Without taking her eyes off Honey, Eloise reached into the fridge, dipped her fingers into the first bowl she came to, scooped out what was inside, and snuffled straight into the palm of her hand without looking. It was mayonnaisy coronation chicken and impossible to eat neatly with her fingers.

She licked her fingers and went in for more. Honey paused, then did the same thing, reaching into the fridge without looking and taking out a plate of sliced avocado. She stuffed some neat green slices into her mouth, then pushed a couple at Eloise, who was still eating the chicken, and when Honey's fingers pushed her mouth open and curried mayonnaise and currants spurted through her teeth they both started to laugh.

Honey popped open one of the many bottles of champagne lying in wait on the top shelf, and they both opened their mouths like baby birds to gulp the light bubbly liquid before returning to their crazy game.

When the tomato and chopped chilli couscous came out, though, the competition started in earnest. Honey shook her head, but Eloise forced her lips apart and pushed the food inside, laughing as Honey winced and squealed at the heat of the chilli and tipped a carton of cranberry juice down her throat to quench the fire.

'Tastes so much better when there's no one else around,' remarked Honey. There was strawberry and cranberry juice all down her chin. She swiped hopelessly at it with the hem of her dress, lifting it right up to reveal her long bare legs and tiny pink thong.

'You've missed a bit,' Eloise giggled, and leant forward to lick the juice off Honey's chin. Her tongue swiped upwards and touched Honey's mouth, which dropped open with surprise. They froze, mouth to mouth, eyes wide and staring in the bright light and buzzing cold of the fridge.

Eloise blushed and drew away, scrabbling quickly in the fridge again to hide her confusion, expecting Honey to scramble to her feet and flounce off. But without a word Honey took a raspberry out of another punnet with her teeth and knelt forwards, nudging the fruit against Eloise's mouth. Eloise took it, her lips once again brushing Honey's. She sank her teeth into it to let the juice burst out, but Honey didn't move away, left her mouth resting against Eloise's as she finished the fruit, and then suddenly they were kissing, strawberry and raspberry juice and milk and tomatoes and champagne dribbling down their necks into their flimsy dresses as they crawled closer to each other and slipped about in the mess on the floor.

Honey's lips were like warm wet cushions, but the rest of her was light and dainty as a fairy. They knelt face to face, smearing more juice and food up each other's shoulders and cheeks, and then Eloise took hold of Honey to draw her closer.

Reaching round her was easy, she was so slim, and there it was again. A kick deep in her groin as Honey's nipples poked through her silky shift dress against Eloise's, their breasts squashing against each other. How had Eloise lived 20 odd years without realising that embracing another woman was like playing with yourself, only infinitely more exciting? That women were soft, warm, scented, damp, forbidden, and goddamn sexy!

Honey was returning the embrace now, putting her arms round Eloise.

'I didn't think I was ever going to get you on your own,' Honey whispered, her breath shivering across Eloise's cheek. 'My family all wanted a piece of you. I saw them.'

Eloise pulled away slightly. 'What did you see? Exactly?'

'I wasn't peeping, honest!' Honey blushed, dropping her hands from Eloise's arms. 'But I did see Freddy and Rick

126

slouching into your room on Friday night. I was so jealous.'

'Yeah, Freddy's gorgeous, isn't he? The best. So young and hunky, and hung like a donkey!' Eloise giggled, tucking Honey's hair behind her ear. 'You should have joined us.'

'Oh God, like a shot if my brother wasn't in there.' Honey took another swig of champagne and handed the bottle to Eloise. 'When I saw you coming into the dining room with Mimi I knew what she'd done to you. Like, woken you up?'

'Did it really show that much?' Eloise drank from the bottle, aware that Honey's saliva was still on the rim. 'It was the first time I'd ever been with a woman.'

Honey was silent for a moment. 'I made out with girls at school. Well, kissed them, anyway.'

Eloise licked cream off her fingers. 'So you'll know how good it felt.'

Honey nodded. 'They were all so pretty. We used to have midnight feasts, you know, a bit like this. There was a group of sixth formers who used to let us smoke in their rooms. And we'd lie on the bed in our nighties and listen to the pop charts and sometimes they had marijuana and you know how horny that makes you.'

Eloise was staring at Honey's mouth as she spoke. It was like a magnet pulling her towards those bee-stung lips. 'What happened?'

'Well, they lay on the beds with us. I had two girls on the bed with me, they were prefects actually, and they were actually kissing each other, putting their hands up each other's nighties, stroking their thighs, pushing their fingers up into their, you know, pussies, and I thought they wanted me to go, stop playing gooseberry, but then they rolled on top of me and started kissing me and touching me, too, and there was a lot of panting and gasping and one of them, there were so many fingers I don't know who, one of them finger fucked me till I came.'

Honey stopped talking and looked down. Such long

eyelashes. Eloise was dizzy with holding her breath. Then Honey looked up again, her blue eyes so like her brothers' eyes. But Rick and Jake were a couple of young stags. Their sister was half kitten, half tiger, with those blazing eyes and that big wet waiting mouth.

'We've got all night,' Eloise heard herself say into the silence. 'So why don't you show me.'

She tangled her fingers in Honey's silky hair, messing it up with her sticky fingers, and kissed her again, parting her soft lips with her tongue. Honey didn't resist. She kind of swooned into Eloise's arms and this time her tongue flicked out, smaller than a man's, so gentle and hesitant, and Eloise swirled her own tongue round it, showing her how gentle this could be, and as they breathed into each other's faces and tangled their tongues more forcefully, they started pulling at each other's clothes.

Eloise pulled Honey's little dress off, and there were her breasts, no bra, her tits just dropping like blossom into her hands, so adorable that Eloise nearly came there and then just feeling them, she had on idea how wet she was already and how ready, she fondled them until she felt Honey shiver and push against her, and Eloise realised she was the older woman here, the teacher and guide.

She dipped her finger into a ramekin of chocolate mousse and put a blob on each stiff nipple, making Honey shiver and chuckle with the cold, then she bent down to kiss Honey's breasts, moving her mouth round the edge, circling round the nipple, not actually touching it, all the time fearing the flinch of resistance, for Honey to push her off with a horrified gasp of disgust, but instead she just arched herself more invitingly. Eloise smeared more mousse on to her, watching her all the time, then licked it slowly off one rosy nipple, feeling it like a little nut amongst the gooey chocolate. Honey didn't move, simply closed close her eyes in rapture, and as Eloise licked clean the other nipple her own grew rock hard with excitement.

This was so wild. Eloise pushed Honey down on to the hard kitchen floor and then peeled off her own dress while Honey watched her, and then Eloise bent down and started licking and sucking Honey's cute nipples again until she was moaning and tugging at Eloise's hair, and Eloise realised how hungry she was to taste every inch of this girl, so she moved her mouth down over her flat stomach, down to the pink thong, easily ripped it aside to reveal her neat pussy, the lips plump and sweet, a line of moisture oozing between them

On impulse she dipped her hand into the chocolate mousse again, smeared all over Honey's pussy, and then she started to lick it off, running her tongue over those sex lips, finally daring to run her tongue up between them.

'Oh, fuck, they never went this far, oh, yes!'

Instantly Honey opened her legs wider for Eloise, arched her back, rubbed and squeezed her own breasts as Eloise lifted her bottom and pushed her pussy into her face, sniffing and tasting the moisture as she licked at her, breathing in the sharp aroma of arousal coming off her cunt.

Honey wrapped her thighs round Eloise's head and moaned as Eloise sucked at her red clit, fingers simply holding her bottom up so that she was tightly pressed against her face, doing everything with her tongue, probably stinging Honey's tender pussy with the chilli juices in her mouth, sucking rougher now, licking then sucking then pushing her tongue right up into the girl's cunt like a mini cock again and again until she screeched and bucked, slamming against the hard floor, wrapping her thighs round Eloise's head as she licked her to climax.

There was a pause, punctuated only by a hiccup from the fridge.

'That better than the girls at school?' Eloise asked quietly, realising that she wanted to be the best thing Honey had ever had.

'Mind-blowingly better.' Honey raised herself up on her

elbows. 'Hey. You haven't seen our summer house yet, have you?' She held out her hand. 'You said we had all night. Let's spend the night in there, far away from prying eyes.'

They grabbed the champagne and ran out across the dark lawn striped with moonlight, into the wooden pavilion by the river. The little hut was warm from the sun beating down on it all day, and welcoming with the lanterns and candles Honey lit. The music started to murmur out of her iPod, the bottles of wine and beer and cakes and fruit on plates scattered on the floor.

'Our own midnight feast,' Honey giggled.

They fell on to a heap of enormous cushions and after cramming more food and drink into each other's mouths they started to kiss once again, passionately and brazenly, tongues licking and pushing really greedily now, hands running roughly and insistently over each other's soft feminine skin, and soon Eloise had Honey's silky head down between her breasts, pushed her hot, aching nipples at her rosebud mouth, urged her to suckle. The girl's tongue came out as she hesitated, a flush flooding her cheeks, and then she nibbled shyly at one nipple, flicked her tongue over it, smiled to see the way it grew hard and dark in response.

'Go on, darling, go on, suck me, bite me, it's such a gorgeous feeling, you'll see–'

Honey tried again, tightening her lips round the bud this time and starting to suck, and as their hands roved over each other, in between each other's legs, Eloise thought she might burst there and then watching that lovely young head suckling at her. She lay down beside Honey as she sucked, touching herself and seeing how wet and sticky her pussy was, and then she took a chance.

She pushed Honey gently back on the cushions, kissing her all the while, letting her breasts hang there for Honey to suck, and then she dared herself to push herself on to Honey's face. There was a muffled squeal underneath her, and then those little hands came up and pulled Eloise's

130

bottom, pulled her pussy into her face, and then the licking started. Soft, almost feathery caresses over her pussy lips, which were pulsing quietly with excitement, and then the wet tip of Honey's tongue flicking up Eloise's wet crack then smoothing itself flat over the swollen lips.

Eloise's head was spinning. She stared out of the window at the trees black against the indigo London sky, heard the sirens going about their business in the distance, a train rattling over a bridge somewhere, and the lights of other houses twinkling on the swaying river.

If only the people in the planes, the trains, the houses, could see into this little den, the two girls writhing on the sumptuous cushions, pleasuring each other for the very first time, the blonde silky head moving between the taut white thighs of the older girl while the older girl struggled to compose herself, trying to stay upright, weak with the effort of not coming all over her little playmate's face.

Honey's mouth and lips were strumming Eloise expertly as if she was a musical instrument. Eloise spread her legs a little further, opening herself to more intense pleasure, seeing herself as those far away travellers or neighbours might see her. A young woman sitting on a younger woman's face, framed through the wooden windows like a still for them all to see.

She pushed herself harder on to Honey's face. She could hear Honey whispering something.

'No, I'm not letting you stop. Not now.'

'I was saying you taste so sweet, Eloise.'

Eloise moaned and strained, pressing down as Honey's tongue lapped faster, like the eager kitten she was, and the thought of her as a little furry pet sizzled through Eloise, sensations sizzling in her cunt as Honey's mouth seemed to devour her entire pussy. Her tongue probed more confidently, forcing its way further in, then pulling back so that Eloise ground herself harder into Honey's face.

Honey was a quick learner. Her tongue flicked

mercilessly now at Eloise's clitoris and she started to jerk frantically. Honey was still sucking, still flicking, her tongue building up the pressure as Eloise rocked back and forth, opening her legs still wider so that she was a proper feast for Miss Honey.

She could hear Honey's saliva mingling with her own pussy juice. She had stopped circling and sucking the burning clit and her tongue was now pushing up inside Eloise's cunt, flicking from side to side, sliding over the clit as it thrust in and out. Eloise rocked faster, her cunt and lips and clit rubbing against Honey's tongue and nose and chin, her hips bucking more wildly.

'This OK, Honey? Not hurting you, am I?' she whispered, afraid she might be suffocating the girl, but Honey shook her head and dug her nails sharply into Eloise's bottom to shut her up.

An aeroplane lowered itself from the night sky as if might land flat on its belly on the rooftops. Eloise thought vaguely of this girl's brothers, flying to opposite ends of the globe, off to see other sights, those gorgeous cocks of theirs off to fuck other women. Honey was working her into a final frenzy now, her mouth and tongue lapping frantically, and here it came.

Eloise scrabbled on the cushions, drew her hips back in a final glorious convulsion and her cunt, her whole body drew in on itself, grew tight as she started to come, pushing herself into Honey's face, smearing her with her juices, rubbing herself on and on over her face until she started to scream with pleasure and jerked and writhed, her pussy clenching tight to keep in the sensation as long as possible.

And then the night went on, the two of them sucking and fingering each other on those soft cushions, until eventually they fell asleep in each other's arms as a new dawn streaked the sky.

Chapter Seven

SO HER COMMISSION WAS pretty much done.

Eloise was woken up by church bells ringing in the distance and the morning sun peering through the arched, ivy-clad windows of the pavilion. She took a couple more pictures of a naked sleeping Honey looking like something out of a Midsummer Night's Dream, golden hair spread over the velvet cushions, arms wide in greeting, legs crooked over Eloise's as if she wanted to keep her there, lips pouting in sleep.

Somehow Eloise knew she'd be back to this place. Just as soon as this family were reunited. Or even better, when they were all split into individual parts that Eloise might savour at leisure, one by one.

But now she had to go home.

She tiptoed into the kitchen. The mess had been cleaned up. Not a trace of strawberry, chilli or trifle remained on the floor. Only her own dress, draped accusingly over one of the chairs, and Honey's bright pink thong, ripped off by Eloise's teeth, kicked, or hidden, under the wine rack.

As she reached the top of the stairs she heard a groan coming from Mimi's bedroom. The door at the end of the landing was ajar. She barely had to think about pushing it open and walking right on in. This house felt like her house. These people were all hers to play with.

She could hear the splashing of the shower. There was a squeaking of flesh on glass, and then another groan. She crept past the huge, rumpled bed towards the bathroom.

The transparent walls of the shower unit were steamed

up, but she could see them give slightly from inside, fleshy-pink shapes flattening against the soap-streaked panels, then being sucked away again. There was some kind of struggle going on.

'Are you all right in there, Mimi?'

There was a snorting giggle in response, and a man's low laugh. Eloise stopped. They were both in there. Above the basin there was a big round chrome mirror shaped like a ship's porthole and reflected in it she could see Mimi's curved, rump, swaying slightly. As she stared, Mimi turned towards the mirror, staggering slightly on the slippery tiles, and parted her legs.

Cedric was kneeling between her legs, streaked by water and soap bubbles. He grabbed at Mimi's thighs and pulled them wide, revealing her waxed secret pussy lips nestled there, plump and open and lined with bright pink. Eloise took a step backwards. She ought to get out of here. But the floorboard creaked as she tried to make her getaway.

Then Cedric buried his face between Mimi's legs and Eloise sat down heavily on the edge of the bed, her throat tightening. As Cedric's nose and mouth made contact with Mimi's cunt, Eloise's hand copied what he was doing, sliding straight down towards her pussy. It was sticky from Honey's little fingers, her mouth and tongue, but also freshly damp from excitement at the sight of Cedric and Mimi making out in the shower.

Now Cedric's head was moving slowly up and down, and Mimi was shaking with growing pleasure. He withdrew for a moment. He pulled her plump labia further apart so that her pink delicacies peeped out. His long red tongue curled out as if he was about to lick a particularly delicious ice cream. Eloise's finger followed suit, stroking up her own crack as she watched.

Cedric fastened his mouth on Mimi's snatch and their bodies were glossy with water and soap in the steamy little room. It was difficult to work out what was real and what

134

was reflected. Eloise fell back against the bathroom wall, desire ripping through her. She could almost feel Cedric licking her now. Her hands rubbed more frantically, wishing it was his tongue, or Mimi's, or Honey's, that was doing this to her, straining to scale that desperate point, just out of reach.

But the movement must have flashed in the mirror, because suddenly Mimi looked round and her reflected eyes met Eloise's. Mimi smiled, red lips spreading into a filthy grin wide enough to split her face. She put a finger to her lips as Cedric's tongue pushed into her, inviting Eloise into her world of sensation.

Her eyes held Eloise's for a minute or two longer but then Cedric stood up, He'd seen her, too.He looked at her for a moment, communicating some kind of order.

And so she picked up her camera, and began to shoot.

Mimi took a huge bar of lemon coloured soap and rubbed it energetically between her palms to get the suds and foam going, and then she dropped the soap and took Cedric's erect cock in her hands and started to soap it, tucking the bulging soft tip into one hand and swiping up and down the shaft with the other. Eloise caught it in her viewfinder as it quivered and rose through the bubbles, extending like a telescope, lengthening from his flat stomach, smoothing out the skin, ironing out any wrinkles until it was straight and smooth and even longer than she remembered, emerging strong and proud through the yellow bubbles.

Mimi pulled at it roughly, making it even longer, and lathered the big balls that hung beneath it, his height making the end of his prick jab into her stomach even when she was standing on tiptoes.

Cedric's head rolled back against the shower wall as he kept his eyes on the camera, but his smile slowly faded and his lips dropped open as Mimi moved her hands harder and faster up and down the long, hard shaft, working the soap into a luxurious lather, making his dick jump and pump, and

Eloise moved the focus to Mimi's fingers, dainty but strong on the big cock, sliding back towards his balls, cupping them with one hand while the other travelled further back, up between his buttocks and suddenly her finger darted into his tight butt hole, forcing a reaction from him.

His hands stretched out helplessly and grabbed at Mimi's hips, circling her waist and pulling her right into him so that his cock was jammed upright between her tits and at last they were moving together, joined together again, her pushing her whole torso against him, reaching under him, his balls retracting with his mounting excitement while her finger poked higher and higher up into his tight anus, reaching for the spot where she would tickle and prod and he would jump and scream.

Eloise's knees were shaking, but she couldn't sit down. She came further into the bathroom and saw that Mimi's nipples were hard as they pressed against Cedric, making his penis grow longer, pinned as it was against her. He began to shudder, and suddenly he forced her hands away from him. The bubbles were running away now and his cock was gleaming and clean, bouncing under the needles of water still pounding down.

Both Mimi and Eloise licked their lips, the camera wobbling in Eloise's hands as she tried to regain focus.

Cedric spun Mimi round so roughly that she grabbed on to the chrome shower pipe to avoid crashing over on the slippery, soapy floor. Now he was pressed up behind her. He lifted her so that her feet rested on the little ledge which ran round the base of the shower tray, and then he cupped one large hand under her dripping cunt and parted her sex lips, thrusting his fingers inside her.

Eloise's cunt was contracting wildly with vicarious excitement as Cedric pulled his fingers out of Mimi and parted her legs until she started to rise right off her toes like some kind of living doll. She was practically swinging off the shower rail now, and moved backwards to sit on the tops of his legs which were slightly bent as he grappled her from behind. They'd obviously done this before. It was like a dance. A performance, just for Eloise and her camera.

As he raised his pelvis Mimi lowered her eager cunt to meet the tip of his cock, ready and waiting, hard as iron. She rested her cheek against the panel for a moment, her face rosy with ecstasy, his face frowning with concentration, and it made a fantastic juxtaposition in Eloise's viewfinder, like capturing wildlife on safari, the female practically yawning with easy triumph, the male concentrating on chasing his own pleasure.

Cedric's cock slid right up Mimi, impaling her while the water rained down on them. Inch after glorious inch, Mimi descended slowly and triumphantly until her buttocks were squashed up against his stomach and his huge cock was basically holding her up like some kind of girder. Mimi tried to keep her balance by pressing her hands on the shower wall, Cedric tried to catch her, but they both started to fall.

Mimi let out a shriek as they landed on their hands and knees half in, half out of the shower, and she started to crawl out of the shower, still impaled from behind. Eloise started to lower her camera. Even these two couldn't keep up the acrobatics forever, surely?

But like the alpha male that he was, Cedric wasn't giving up. Glancing again at Eloise, he yanked his wife back against him and started to thrust himself inside her, hardly pulling out at all, just keeping himself right inside so that she was pushed and pulled across the slippery tiles with whatever movement he chose, her hands and knees squeaking with the friction, his hands holding her against him, not needing to do anything more to stimulate her, just letting her tight vagina welcome him in so that they were welded together, the beast with two backs, rocking back and forth on the floor, grinding and thrusting.

Eloise continued shooting as Cedric pumped faster and faster, muttering into his wife's neck, resting his mouth and teeth there while he fucked her and then all at once he lifted her off the ground with the force of his coming and she wiggled her hips from side to side to give herself more friction and then she was obviously coming too as he pulled her right up against him and pumped his juices into her while hers flowed and mingled with the warm rushing water and the ebbing bubbles.

Eloise backed out to return to her room. Lying on her bed she flicked through the photographs. By now there was only the slightest jolt of surprise to see the newest additions. Her with little Honey in the candlelit pavilion, the two girls crawling over each other on the outsize velvet cushions, all apple cheekbones, arched throats, flowing hair – and tongues, kissing, licking, swiping all over. Warmth flooded through her as she realised how determined, how dominant she looked with the other girl. How knowing.

Her shoot just now in the master bedroom was like a silent movie. The Mimi and Cedric Show. Their bodies flowed from frame to frame, arms, legs, faces, mouths, all working towards their climax. She could see it on a loop, playing constantly on a big screen.

Because it was turning her on all over again. She switched off the camera and fingered herself to a climax and then fell into an exhausted sleep.

Chapter Eight

SHE LET HERSELF IN early the following morning before Jake got there, and quickly uploaded her photographs on to the huge computer in his office. She wanted to take another good look and then edit them. Perhaps those other mysterious pictures featuring her being seduced, one by one, by each member of the Epsom family, would simply melt away from the memory disk. Or perhaps they were just part of her fevered imagination.

But everything was there. It couldn't have been some kind of mistake with the self timer. The out of focus, dreamy shots contrasted so sharply with her cool, composed style, but there was nothing accidental about them. In fact the more she looked at them in the cold light of day, the more skilled they obviously were.

So who the hell was the unknown photographer, stalker, ghost, whatever, hiding in the shadows, capturing every intimate sexy moment as she tasted those new people, those new experiences? How had they transferred the images to her camera? Was it one of the family? Unlikely, as they were either with her or on their way to somewhere else.

The post clattered through the letter box, landed with a slap on the doormat, and there, in a smooth white envelope, was the fat cheque Cedric Epsom had promised her. No fevered dream, then.

'You look knackered. Good weekend, was it?'

Jake made her jump, coming up behind her holding a bucket of Cafe Americano.

'I stayed at the Epsoms.'

'The whole weekend?'

'In the end, yes. They wanted me to do a family montage of all their, er, comings and goings.'

She tried to minimise the images on the computer but he slapped her hand away. The computer hummed as the pictures slid past, her clever, artful shots interspersed with the furry, blurry ones: Eloise with Mimi, her astonished face reflected in the Venetian mirror; Eloise with Rick and Freddy on the bedroom rug, Freddy's face ablaze with longing as he waited his turn, then his cock aimed like a javelin about to penetrate her; Jake sucking her nipples on the hot damp riverbank. The pictures all looked suddenly bigger and more graphic, and excruciatingly embarrassing now Jake was staring at them as well.

He gave a long, low whistle. 'Christ, girl, what have they done to you? This isn't a montage – it's a porn film story board only just disguised as art. *The Corruption of Eloise Stokes.* Although God knows you're photogenic when you're naked. Who knew?'

'Ironic coming from the photographer who's been shagging me all these years.' She swallowed. 'So you're not shocked at what they – what I've been getting up to?'

'Shocked? A little. That sex pot ain't the innocent little Elle I know. Jealous? Volcanically so. And I'll show you just how volcanically as soon as we can shut up shop.'

Eloise tried to smile. 'What if Cedric sees these? Me with his wife, well, he'll probably get off on all that lesbian stuff, seen it all before, but me with his kids? They're all grown up, but, Christ, he'll probably sue me for assault! And worst of all he'll stop his bloody cheque!'

'He won't see the out of focus pictures.'

She frowned. 'How can you be so sure?'

'Relax and come here, gorgeous. You're still my girl. You obviously haven't missed me, but I've missed you.' Jake kissed her slowly, knowing that it would shut her up, melt her, bring her back to him. Then he pushed her down roughly onto the battered leather sofa. 'Come on, baby. Do it to me, like you did it to those lucky Epsoms.'

His mouth used to be so gentle, so familiar. As he'd pointed out before, he was the only lover she'd ever had. Before the bruises, the bite on her neck, her aching cunt, her sore nipples, before she collected all those indelible signs of a debauched weekend.

'Actually, I missed you too, Jake. Didn't think I would, but I thought about you.'

'In amongst all that dazzling wealth and beauty?' He laughed a little harshly. 'OK. Show me how much you missed me.'

He pushed her down on to her hands and knees and yanked her little skirt up over her bottom.

'Hey, wind it in!' she squealed furiously. 'What have I done wrong?'

'Made like some nympho with that entire family behind my back, that's what. And it's all there on film, every fuck, every wriggle, every lick, and oh yes, they've paid you, so what does that make you, hmm?'

'They paid me for my work, not my–'

'A hooker, that's what. Those Epsoms took my girl, and gave me back a whore!'

Her astonished protest was silenced by Jake slapping her hard on the bottom. She twisted round, about to unleash a torrent of enraged abuse before scratching his eyes out, but he just flipped her round and slapped her again. This time the stinging of the blow rooted her to the spot. The heat of it radiated from his handprint and a strange, surprising pleasure seared through her.

'Well, if *I'm* a whore,' she hissed, 'you've turned into some kind of pervert!'

He slapped her again, making the soft flesh on her butt ripple. 'They wanted to get you into their mansion, and they wanted to seduce you. All of them. And they are all experts. You can see it from the pictures. You loved every minute of it!'

'They wanted my pictures, that's why I was there, but yes. I loved it. Once it started, I never wanted that weekend to end. So what?'

She struggled to get back into a more dignified position, but he pushed her back down.

'You're a horny little slut, that's what, and you need punishing.'

She tipped her head back, laughing with disbelief, but he slapped her again and this time her whole body shivered with new, low-down excitement at the manic way he was behaving. Like he'd been taken over by the spirit of someone else. Cedric Epsom, perhaps. And despite, or because of that, the feel of her buttocks flinching under his hand, the way the harshness of the slap softened into a wicked warmth, really turned her on.

She glanced over her shoulder. 'You just wish you were there, watching me with Mimi, teasing those boys in my bedroom, deflowering young Jake, practising my new lezzie techniques on the cute, soft Honey – and by the way you know Cedric fucked me in his office chair that day, right in front of the window where half the City could see?'

'Yeah. I knew that, too. And yeah, I've told you I'm mad with jealousy. Happy now? I'm jealous, because I love you, and you're mine, and I'm going to keep it that way.' Jake ran his hands over her bottom, gripping her hips. He touched her sore cheeks, tracing the star shape where he had slapped her.

'I told you before, and this weekend has proved it.' She wriggled furiously, trying to get away. 'I'm not yours, or anyone's.'

'Quite the reverse, because here you are, come right back to me. You know I'm right, Eloise. I'm the only guy for you.' He stroked her buttocks almost absently, then slid his hand round to touch her pussy. 'You're creaming yourself, which proves it. So if it's new experiences you're after, I'll

142

show you something new.'

She couldn't deny it. Her mild mannered Jake was on a mission. Her cunt was clenching now with a sickly dark desire as he pushed his fingers inside her. She started to grind down to push them further in, but suddenly he pulled away, unzipped his jeans and took his cock out of his trousers. They both watched it grow and harden as he squeezed it in the palm of his hand then opened his fingers to show her how big it was.

'Go on then, lover. Fuck me if it makes you feel good,' she hissed like a little witch.

Outside someone knocked at the gallery door. It was well past opening time.

He just chuckled, and parted her butt cheeks to slide his cock up the crack. Her thighs opened for him and she tilted her damp pussy hopefully towards him, but he went on nudging his cock at her arse hole. She swore and jerked with shock but he kept tight hold of her hips and pushed harder against the little hole as it resisted, closed up against him like a fist, then with a little pop it started to give, and open, to let him in, and though it felt sore as he entered it also felt incredible. Hot, tight, really dirty, and as his cock bumped over the stubborn little ring and slid into that space, filling her right up, her body closed eagerly round him, sucking him in.

Another knock at the door, the rumble of a taxi pulling away.

Now Jake was pushing harder, not too roughly, but filling her up with fire. She was afraid she might split open, but her body started to welcome him, fit him in, and then she was moving with him, his familiar body warm as he pulled her back against his stomach. Her hands rubbed at her aching pussy as he started to thrust his way right up, feeling huge inside that tight private space.

She pushed back against him, the dirty excitement rising to fever pitch. This didn't feel like Jake at all. It was like

143

having another new Epsom lover. And then he was pumping harder and harder and it hurt but deliciously so and as he started to come she felt her body clench tight round him and she rubbed her fingers quickly over her clit and she was coming, too, screaming, her hand rubbing on her pussy and his cock thrusting up her arse, teaching her something new all right, his balls banging against her bottom, and her knees squeaking crazily on the leather sofa.

'I heard about you from Cedric Epsom.'

The man who had arrived by taxi had waited patiently on the doorstep for them to, well, finish fucking, and now he was commissioning her to come up to Edinburgh later that month to photograph him in and his dance troupe at work and play during the Fringe. As they talked she was aware of Jake crashing about in the gallery behind her, hanging new pictures.

'That's a great opportunity. Thank you,' she said, taking his advance cash for her travel expenses up to Scotland. 'But my work for Mr Epsom hasn't even been printed yet, let alone shown to him or exhibited, so I don't know how–'

'Oh, the word is out, believe me, and if that one your boss has just hung on the wall behind you is anything to go by, then your work will be going like hot cakes by the end of the Fringe.'

She saw him out of the door then turned, assuming he meant one of her classic works. But there, already framed and in pride of place was a slightly out of focus, enormous picture of her and Honey sprawled on the velvet cushions in the riverside pavilion as the dawn rose last Sunday morning, eyes fluttering closed with fatigue, hands resting on each other's naked breasts.

'You see? I was there all along,' Jake said, kissing Eloise on the neck, right where it was bruised with those vampire bites.

The Highest Bidder
by Sommer Marsden

Chapter One

'ONE, TWO, THREE, FOUR, five ...' Casey blew out a huge breath to steady her nerves and pushed her hands into her hair.

In a moment she was going to start screaming.

'But aren't we supposed to have–'

'Six!' Casey snapped. Then she felt bad and patted her friend's hand. 'Sorry, Annie.'

'No problem, kid.' Annie signalled the waiter by shaking her iced tea glass at him. 'What happened to our sixth?'

Casey rifled the papers in front of her and finally found him. 'Lester Smith – yes – Smith was ...' She shuffled through the pile. She'd gotten a notice on one of the attendees at some point and, oh, yeah, here it was. '... Arrested,' she finished with a disgusted grunt. 'And is being held. And will not be out in time for the charity auction.'

'As if we could *give* him away!' Annie giggled.

The waiter brought the iced tea pitcher and topped her off. She glanced up with a huge smile and her big blue eyes and her swingy brown hair and said, 'Thanks, doll. Now how would you like us to sell you?'

The waiter – whose name tag read Benjamin – blinked furiously and turned an alarming shade of tomato. 'Excuse me?'

'Oh, don't worry. Not a man-whore or anything,' Annie said, waving her hand.

Casey took the moment to cradle her aching head in her hands. Dear God. 'Annie ...' she whispered.

'It's for charity, Benjamin. And you are too cute.'

Casey had to nip it in the bud. She looked up and smiled at the blushing boy. 'How old are you, Benjamin?'

'Seventeen, ma'am.'

Annie *hmphed* quietly but then laughed.

'When will you be eighteen?'

'This summer.'

'Case closed,' Casey said. 'You're too young. Run like the wind, Ben. Run away from the crazy lady. And can I get the check?'

'Yes – yes, ma'am,' he said and fled. Good boy. He knew wisdom when he heard it.

'Now,' she said, turning to her friend, 'Can you please help me find a non-law-breaking man to fill in this space? You have to know men. You're single and hot and all that jazz.'

'You are too.' Annie looked her dead in the eye – she was getting that stubborn look again.

'I'm–'

'Brendan has been gone for over a year,' Annie said softly.

'I know that. And I'm–'

'If you say *fine* I will totally rip a chunk of your hair out,' Annie said conversationally.

Casey chewed her lip. Her friend was right but she didn't want to have this conversation. 'Being a widow is different than being broken up with,' she said.

'Of course it is!' Annie grabbed her hand and squeezed it. 'But you are gorgeous and funny and smart as hell. You are vibrant and young and Christ, Case, if anyone would want you to be happy it'd be Brendan.'

'Enough,' she said, pulling her hand away.

Annie caught the tone and was a good enough friend to stop talking. They took the check and Casey paid. This charity event to benefit diabetes was all she cared about right now. Type 1 had taken her husband; the least she could do was attempt to keep it from taking someone else's spouse. 'Now ... we really need a sixth man. Each team provides six for a total of eighteen. A dozen and a half bachelors for charity,' she laughed. 'Work your magic, Annie.'

Annie rolled her eyes but said, 'Fine. Fine. I'll see what I can do.'

Casey didn't say it, but she needed Annie to do it because she didn't know any single men. She hadn't paid a lick of attention to a man besides her own in years. And now he was gone she was following the same pattern.

So what if she was lonely?

'His name is Nick Murphy. And he's hot.'

Casey glanced at her intake form for the bachelor participants. 'I do not see a box marked "hot".'

'Well, add it.'

'How tall?'

'Why don't you just wait until he's here?' Annie sighed.

'How tall?' Casey was so stressed she felt like she might pop a blood vessel. This auction was for a good cause but she was such a perfectionist it was giving her hives. This guy was new and they had to practice. There was a fine line between fun and cheesy and she wanted to make sure the auction came off as fun and flirty and definitely worth the money.

'Six three.'

Casey felt her mouth go dry. What the hell was that? She glanced up at Annie who was now smirking. 'Pardon?'

'Six. Three. Did I stutter?' Annie said.

Casey's cheeks went hot and she shook her head. 'Don't be such a brat. How much does he weigh do you think?'

147

Annie shrugged. 'Don't know. Two hundred? Plus most of it's muscle. And I bet a good portion of it is between his le–'

'Eyes!' Casey barked.

'What?'

'Eyes,' she sighed. For some reason talking about this new guy was making her feel … flirty? No. Not flirty. She was lying to herself. Horny.

It was making her horny. Which she hadn't been in ages.

Which was completely insane.

'Two,' Annie said.

A bark of laughter shot out of Casey before she could stifle it and she clapped a hand over her mouth. Some of the other women volunteers turned to see what was going on. Thankfully none of the bachelors had arrived yet.

'Annie,' she hissed between her fingers.

'Blue,' Annie sighed.

'Hair?' Casey went on, ignoring her racing pulse. It made no sense. How did one get turned on by discussing a stranger?

'Yes?' Annie glanced out the front window.

'What colour!' Casey said and actually stomped her foot.

'Whoa, you are uptight. You know what you need–'

'To know his hair colour,' Casey said.

'Black. And no. You need a good hard …' She leaned in and said it. Casey didn't think she'd say it, but she did. 'Fuck.'

'Annie, you are terrible. I just can't–' Casey turned, upset by her friend's blunt words. But more upset by the fact that she thought she might be right. She stumbled, twisted an ankle and promptly slammed into a wall. Who wasn't actually a wall.

'Hi,' he said, looking down at her.

Tall, black hair, blue eyes … and huge, did she say that part?

'Hi,' Casey said and tried to stand up. She promptly

148

winced when her ankle gave her a sharp jab of pain.

'You OK?'

'Fine.' She tried to stand up tall again and again but every time she winced and hissed and bent her knees.

'I don't think you are,' the giant said.

He had his hands on her waist to steady her and Casey swore she could feel a baking heat from his palms all around her waist, up her back, into her chest and yes, Jesus Pleasus, into her pelvis. Her pussy gave a wet flex even as her heartbeat doubled in speed and Casey was pretty damn sure someone had turned the heat up.

'I am,' she lied. But on the final try, the jab of pain became a punch and she yelped.

'Yeah, I don't know you but you're lying,' he said and scooped her up before she could tell him no.

Annie gave a snort and said, 'Oh yeah, Casey, this is Nick Murphy. Nick, this is Casey Briggs. And there's a room in the back marked Lounge. Take her back there and I'll find an ice pack.'

Nick nodded and started toward the back. Casey held her breath. Why was she holding it? So she couldn't smell him. The look of him was one thing, the feel of his hands on her – on her ass no less – was another. A very distracting other thing. But the smell of him, that she picked up on first contact was so overwhelming she was trying not to inhale. Fresh cut wood, fall leaves, nutmeg. He smelled like fall and cosy things and, God help her, sex.

He smelled like sex. And no one had smelled like sex to Casey for a very long time.

Chapter Two

'IS HERE GOOD?'

Casey blinked and realised how stupid she must look. She'd been too busy trying to focus her attention against the smell of him, the feel of him, and truly ... the look of him, to actually hear him.

'What?'

Nick nodded to a chaise longue and said, 'Is here good?'

He smiled at her and her stomach tumbled with heat, something lower did too. Casey suffered a brief but vivid flash of that dark head between her thighs. That generous mouth licking and kissing and sucking ... she sighed out loud. When she heard it, her eyes went wide.

Nick smiled at her. Blue eyes never leaving her blushing face. 'You OK?'

Just trying not to imagine your startling blue eyes looking up at me as you go down on me ...

'Fine. Totally. And here is fine, too. I'm sure I'm heavy. Your back is probably breaking. And ...'

Why was she babbling? She clamped her lips together to keep from speaking any more nonsense. Nick sat her down gently and pulled a folding chair to the foot of the chaise.

'You're not heavy at all. I like your hair.' Now he blushed.

Casey touched her hair as if she'd never encountered it before. Never mind the dirty blond mass was constantly the bane of her existence. Today she'd twisted it up into an intricate messy knot and speared it with a hair pick Brendan had given her once upon a time. When she felt the smooth,

150

carved teak under her fingertips she had a sudden and horrible stab of guilt.

Annie walked in, caught the look of irrational guilt and yelled, 'Stop!'

Nick started and said, 'What? What do you mean stop, Annie?'

'I meant, um ...' Her friend gave her the evil eye when Nick turned back to Casey. 'To stop worrying. I have the ice!'

She practically threw it at Nick, who plucked it from the air as if performing a magic trick. He took Casey's foot and gently worked the straps on her heel. 'Sorry, we should get it out of this heel in case it swells. Am I hurting you?'

Casey heard Annie chuckle. She was watching intently and Casey could feel – as horrifying as it was – the look of arousal on her own face. The feel of his hands on her skin – soothing and ever so gentle – had her tongue feeling two sizes too big. And her panties felt about two sizes too small.

'Yeah, she looks in agony,' Annie said. 'I'll go check in the arrivals.'

'Oh, no, wait!' Casey said, feeling anxiety in her gut like a lance.

'You'll be fiiii-iiiine,' Annie trilled over her shoulder and tossed her a finger wave.

Bitch. Deserter. Traitor!

'How does this feel?' Nick now had her foot between his legs. He was rubbing the spot that had been painful and she barely felt a twinge.

'Ummmm,' she said and then realised how close to a moan that was.

He glanced up and smiled and her stomach dropped like she was free falling.

'Can you flex it?'

Casey pointed her toe and this time they both froze. When their eyes met she couldn't read him, but she was sure that *she* looked mortified.

151

She had just nudged her toes against his crotch. And if she wasn't hallucinating – which she might be – he was getting hard. 'I'm so sorry,' she said.

But she didn't move her foot.

Move your foot! Move. Your. Foot. Oh my God, woman, move your foot.

So she moved her foot ... by pointing it further and rubbing the very distinct erection that now resided here.

'I'm not,' he blurted. When he looked away, looking as embarrassed as she was, but also, yes, turned on, she felt a tiny rush of confidence.

'I didn't mean to ... but when I ... when I ...'

'When you?'

This time his stare was direct. He'd gathered his wits and that meant hers fled.

'I just ... was surprised and well, flattered and oh my God, I'm sorry.' She tried to stand but he took one big hand and gently forced her back.

'Look, toe foreplay or not, there is some swelling so just sit here for a bit with the ice on. It's OK. I'm sorry I ... *reacted.*'

'Don't be,' she said. 'But hey, you ...' Time to change the subject. 'You look worried. Did my friend blackmail you into being here or what?'

His fingers encircled her ankle and she watched him, somewhat mesmerized, as his fingers crept a little higher up her leg. His gaze was pinned to the place where her skirt ended. Casey almost gasped when she felt a small rush of fluid between her legs. Her panties were now officially wet.

And you brain has officially shut down ...

'I am nervous,' he said, leaning in. His eyes danced from her thighs to her face and back again. Casey found herself both hotter than hell and flattered beyond all belief. How long had it been since a man had looked at her that way?

She couldn't remember or hadn't noticed.

Without really thinking she moved her toes again and, for

just a fluttering instant, his hand gripped her leg tighter. She felt the resounding surge of heat as it coursed up her leg to nestle in her sex.

'Why?' Her voice was barely a whisper.

He smiled at her, smoothing his fingertips along her skin so that her skin pebbled in goose flesh. 'I'm afraid no one will want me. You know ... no one will bid on me. And I won't earn any money for charity and ...' He shrugged, big shoulders rising and falling under his navy blue tee. He wore pale smoke blue chinos and athletic shoes. And that hair and those eyes combined with that body made a hell of a package.

A nervous giggle surged up out of her and she clamped a hand over her mouth. 'You?' Casey finally said. '*You* are worried that no one will want to buy you?'

He nodded. She flexed her toe and his eyelids fluttered. What a rush of power that brought and it hadn't escaped her notice that what was under her foot was ... sizeable. Very sizeable. And that was saying something because being with Brendan hadn't been anything to complain about.

Another stab of guilt at the thought of her dead husband. 'So what do you do?' she barrelled on.

'That's it. All these men who are being auctioned are doctors or lawyers or heirs to great fortunes.' He was absentmindedly stroking her leg.

Casey had to shift due to the pound of her own pulse in her cunt. If she didn't get herself under control she was going to launch herself at him and maul him. It had been over a year since she'd had sex. She felt every moment of that time when he touched her.

'And you?' she prodded.

'I refurbish. Furniture. Sometimes buildings. They're movers and shakers and I ... well, I deal in nostalgia, for the most part.'

She felt a prick of tears in her eyes and swallowed hard to ward them off. 'I think that's ... lovely,' she said. 'I'd better get back. Lots of work to do.' At his warning, she stood slowly. When he was sure she was stable, he stood.

'Don't worry,' Casey said, patting his arm. My gosh, it was a big arm. 'Women will bid on you. Trust me on this.'

It was so unexpected. He leaned in to give her a friendly peck on the cheek, murmuring 'Thanks. I feel a lot better.'

But when he got closer, it changed. The energy, the feel of it, Casey saw it happening as if in slow motion but couldn't stop herself or him. Nick's lips brushed hers and his hands found her hips and she parted her lips for him thinking how fucking easy she was all of a sudden … and how great it was.

The kiss was deep and slow and so sexy her toes curled, especially the foot that was still shoeless.

'That was very unprofessional of me,' she gasped.

'And very forward of me,' he said. But he was studying her with that piercing cool gaze.

Was it inappropriate to want to push him back on the chaise longue, hike up her skirt and climb aboard? Yes. Yes, it was. Casey clenched her fists and her thighs. The second was a bad idea because she pushed herself so very close to the verge of orgasm, it was insane.

'I have to go!' she gasped, hurrying as fast as possible on a bum ankle. 'I hear Annie calling me.'

Total lie. When she got out there, Annie turned to face her and said, 'Why are you here? Shouldn't you be getting your smooch on with Nick?'

'You did this on purpose, didn't you?'

'Me?' Annie batted her eyelashes, all innocence and total bullshit.

Casey snatched the clipboard. 'Yes, you.'

When Nick came out to stand with the other bachelors for rehearsal she felt her heart wedge its way into her throat. When he smiled at her, it dropped way down in her gut. And other parts of her wanted her to march over there and kiss him again.

154

* * *

Nick knew her deal. Annie had told him that Casey Briggs was a widow. He had expected a nice, attractive, maybe a little sad woman trying to do something good. What he had not expected was a tall, willowy, honey blonde with sparkling brown eyes and a nervous way about her that made him want to grab her shoulders and kiss her.

And then of course the surprise "foot job" and her reaction – part horrification, part amusement – had sealed the deal of his attraction.

Now he stood in a line of good-looking men who probably made about six (or sixty) times what he made per year. And she stood there assessing them. Nick couldn't help but feel less than. He wasn't a successful doctor or lawyer, he wasn't a country club member, he wasn't a bad ass pretty boy. He was a refurbisher who was doing a neighbour – the nosy and ornery Annie – a favour. For charity.

It was a good deed. He'd let it go. There was no chance he had a shot in hell with the gorgeous blushing widow. Her husband had probably been just like these men. And though she'd assured him he was attractive – how could she not given the circumstances? – he wasn't of the same calibre.

Which was a shame. Because that kiss had damn near set his head on fire and the way her long slim toes had run across his cock and the things he'd been thinking ... oh, the things he'd been thinking when she'd done it. She would *really* blush.

Nick had had an extremely detailed image of laying that pretty woman down on the chaise longue and hiking up her snug but proper grey skirt. And stripping down her hose, that he could clearly see due to her hurt ankle and reclining position, were thigh highs. He wondered what colour her panties were and had to bite his own tongue to focus.

No erections in rehearsal, you jack-off ...

When he looked up and she smiled at him, looking away

155

shyly as if remembering the kiss, well, he had to bite his tongue twice as hard to keep himself in line.

Chapter Three

'I'VE BEEN WANTING TO do this all night.' His fingers brushed the front seams of her white blouse and then he touched each pearlescent button. Nick wasn't touching *her* but Casey's whole body responded as if he were.

He took a step into her space and she instinctively backed up a little. He did it again and so did she, until he had her wedged against the counter in the ladies' lounge. His pelvis crushed to hers and she felt that magnificent hard-on again. So this time she let her hand travel the length of it, stroking him so that his eyelids flickered like he was falling asleep. Only he was definitely not falling asleep because he thrust forward gently into her hand.

'I want to take this off you. Can I take this off you, Casey?'

He bent to kiss her, running the rigid tip of his tongue over her earlobe and then down her neck. He hit the sweet spot where her pulse jumped beneath her flesh. When he found it with his tongue, he gently nipped her with his teeth at the exact spot.

'Yes, God, fuck, yes. Take it off.'

That's when she knew she was dreaming. Even dreaming, Casey knew this was where the guilt should come slamming down on her. But it didn't. She simply observed what felt like jolts and jolts of electricity run under her skin, as he undid each button.

'Your fingers shouldn't be able to do that,' she whispered. 'They're too big.'

He didn't answer her, just leaned in, tasting her lips and

157

then pushing his tongue into her mouth so she moaned. Now his hands were on her skirt, hiking it up around her waist. Cool air rushed over her exposed thighs and the skin above her thigh highs rippled with goose bumps. Nick pushed a finger under the leg hole of her panties, breaching the elastic and zeroing in on her engorged clit. She was so sensitive – almost oversensitive – that one small stroke with his fingertip had her clutching his biceps so she didn't fall on her ass.

'Do you really think they're too big?' Nick whispered against her hair. He pushed a thick finger into her pussy and when her fingers dug into his arms and she sort of wobbled, he added a second. 'You're really really wet, Casey.'

Another kiss, delivered with plump and impossibly soft lips. The smell of him filled her head and she sucked in a deep breath to get more. Pushing her body against his hand, not caring if it seemed overzealous, just wanting more contact. More friction and penetration and pleasure.

She dug her fingers deeper and wondered if she was hurting him. But another kiss said no, she wasn't. Not hurting him at all.

Nick nipped her breast through her white blouse, through her tiny silky bra. His "just crooked enough to be sexy" front teeth captured the hard nub and he clamped down hard enough to shoot a frisson of brisk pleasure through her middle, down into her womb. His thumb pressed her clit relentlessly and she found herself grinding up to get more.

'Come for me, Casey. I can feel you want to. You're so damn tight around my fingers.'

He nipped her again and curled his wide fingers and pressed her clit and she could feel it swelling up out of her. A rush-tumble-surge of goodness – so sweet and so long overdue it made her nearly sob with the release of it.

Her cunt seized up around his probing fingers and he kissed her gently, swallowing every single cry that burst out of her as she came.

Her fingers trembled, her nerves high and loud due to the newness of it and the anxiety of a new lover. Casey tried to work the button on his faded out chinos. Finally he laughed, licking a hot trail from her earlobe to her collar bone, the sensation intense. Casey feared her nipples might actually pierce her blouse and the thought made her laugh softly.

'A man doesn't want to hear laughter the first time he's with a woman,' he said, looking down at her. Those blue eyes felt like they were piercing her usual armour of self-control and seeing into her scattered chaotic soul.

'I was laughing at me, not you,' she said, and pushed her hand, still shaking, into his pants. He was so warm against her hand. His skin decadently smooth but hard too. His cock felt good – hot and heavy – in her palm and she curled her fingers around him.

'I won't lie. That feels so good. I've been picturing you touching me since the moment I walked in.'

Casey rose on tiptoes and kissed him, stroking her loose fist up and down the length of his erection until he muttered 'tighter' in her ear. She increased her grip and felt a burst of happiness in her chest when he instinctively – animalistically – thrust into her fist.

She didn't let herself think – dream or not – she pushed his pants down and rested her ass against the wall and said, 'Hurry, before I freak myself out. Which I always manage to do.'

He pressed his cock to her. First just the split of her sex, nudging her nether lips with the heated steel of his erection. He thrust against her outer lips, rubbing her clit with the motion, faux-fucking her until her fingers clawed and plucked aimlessly at his upper body.

Casey wedged her hand between them, relishing the press of their bodies, belly to belly. It had been a long time since she had been intimately pressed against a man. A long, long time since she'd taken a man in hand and nudged her own slick opening with the tip of his cock.

159

'Wait.' He held her firmly and then lowered his mouth to hers. 'I want to be kissing you when I enter you.'

She would have said something clever or sweet, but what he'd just said made her tongue double clutch and yes, stupidly, her eyes swim with tears. So she shut them and kissed him back and felt him inching into her, sliding effortlessly, stretching her and nudging her and – *Ring, ring, ring!*

'No,' she groaned.

Ring, ring, ring!

'Oh fuck, no,' Casey sighed. She felt around on the table for her cell phone. She knew where she was not – with Nick.

Where she happened to be was on her sofa, big socks on, sweats rolled around her ankles, one of Brendan's big work sweatshirts wrapped round her.

'Dirty dreams,' she said to herself, finally snagging the phone with her fingertips. 'Dirty, dirty dreams.'

And it had been because her pussy was thumping merrily with blood and arousal and she felt pretty much on the paper's edge of coming like someone firing a cannon. She opened one eye and hit accept on her phone.

'Hello?'

'You sleeping?' It was Annie. Chipper and hyper – probably jacked up on one of those salted-caramel-mocha-frappalatte things she loved so much.

'I dozed. I took a shower, laid down to watch some show about pumpkin carving and crashed, I guess.'

'You OK, you sound funny?'

'Fine,' Casey said, but she heard her voice crack with emotion.

Damn.

'Hey, girly what's wrong? Are you sure you're–'

Casey was mortified to hear the sob rip out of her. And even more horror-struck when she began weeping in earnest. 'Oh God, I'm sorry. I'll call you back–'

'I thought you said you'd been napping!' Annie

160

squeaked.

'I was.'

'Then what in the world makes you cry like this from sleeping?'

'I had a dream–'

'A nightmare?' Annie said, sounding relieved.

'No! A *dream*. A … um … *dream*-dream.'

Silence. Then a sharp intake of air and then Annie's signature high-pitched giggle.

'A sex dream?'

'Yes, a sex dream. And I … we … I cheated on Brendan,' she sighed and dissolved into tears.

Annie went silent again. Casey heard her sigh.

'Honey, you cannot cheat on him. He's dead. And he would kick your ass six ways to Sunday for beating yourself up over something like … oh, *being human*. Craving companionship and yes, a good thorough lay. It's been over a year. And it's never going to get easier if you don't try.'

'But–'

'Tell me Brendan would want you alone and sad and sexually frustrated.'

'But–'

'Tell me!' Annie demanded in her no-bullshit voice.

Casey sighed – it was a long watery sound – and murmured. 'He wouldn't. He told me to be happy. He urged me to be happy. And to …' She shook her head, warring against more tears.

'And?'

'And to love again,' she said.

'Well, there you go. And I know, honey, it's going to be hard. And probably emotional. And all that bullshit that comes with a loss like this. But it will be worth it in the end. If you're having sexy sex dreams that are provoking this much emotion … honey, you're ready.'

'Whatever, 'Casey said, not wanting to discuss it any more.

161

'Was it about Nick?' Now she could hear Annie smiling.

'What? No!' Even she didn't believe her denial.

'Liar. I saw all the horny sparks flying between you two. He's a good egg,' she said more seriously. 'He might just be the guy to ease you into this whole transitional thing. From lonely widow to woman getting her life back.'

Casey shook her head, uncomfortable with the whole thing. 'No.'

'Come have pizza.'

'No!'

'Have you eaten?'

Her stomach grumbled and she mumbled, 'No.' Defeated. Annie would win this.

'Come have pizza and wine and we'll chat about handsome Nick. And you can tell me all the details of your sexy sex dream!' she squealed and hung up before Casey could respond.

He was hallucinating. When Nick peeked out to see if maybe his Chinese food had arrived – since he was now officially starving – he saw her. Casey. The woman from the auction.

His body responded in the same way it did when he was famished and a burger commercial ran on TV. He wanted what he saw. It was such a visceral reaction he had to take a deep breath and get himself under control.

She had to be here to see Annie – had to, but that didn't change Nick's knee-jerk reaction to seeing her. He grabbed the door knob and yanked the door wide, completely faking his surprise.

'Oh! Hey, there. I thought you were my Chinese food.'

Great way to woo a girl. Lie your ass off ...

She blinked and then covered her mouth. Was it him or were her cheeks suddenly a flaming red? She looked as if he'd jumped her and tackled her to the ground.

'Sorry, did I scare you?'

'N-n-no,' she said. But her eyes were wide and he could see her pulse jumping erratically at her throat. Nick clenched his hands into fists because his first instinct – his urge, really – had been to reach out and put his fingertips to that skin. To feel her blood pumping and rushing at seeing him. Even if it was only because he'd startled her.

She was looking at him strangely. Probably because he was acting like a nut. Her hair was wind-tossed and erratic and eddied around her face like she was underwater. There was a breeze rushing down the long communal hallway because someone had cracked the lone window.

'Are you sure you're OK? Is it your ankle?'

She cocked her head at him as if she were having trouble understanding him. Nick noticed her breathing was laboured like she'd run up the steps, but he'd heard the elevator doors when he saw her coming. So what …

He lost that thought because she was rushing at him. Her hands shoved into his hair and she yanked it accidentally, but hard enough to make his dick hard. 'Sorry, sorry,' she muttered, pressing those sweet warm lips to his.

He didn't know what she was sorry for, didn't care. His gripped her waist tight in his hands to hold her to him and kissed her back. When her wet tongue snaked between his lips and teased his, his cock went from hard to the lethal weapon stage.

Nick was fairly certain that at the moment he could chop wood with his erection. But that wasn't what he wanted to do with it.

Conscience got the better of him and he pulled back long enough to say, 'Hey are you sure you're OK? Are you sure about …' He tore his way from those vibrant brown eyes and trained his gaze on her plump red lips.

'I'm sure. I'm sorry, but yes, I'm sure. Can we …?' She pushed her body entirely to his. He felt the heat and heft of her breasts press to his chest and the warm cleft between her legs. She was wearing severely faded and abused jeans with

163

a hole at the knee and Nick was fairly certain he'd never seen a woman look sexier.

She kissed him again and he almost groaned, hating his conscience.

'Can we what?'

Casey tugged his belt and then touched his hard-on, all the while kissing him wherever she could get her lips. Her tongue darted out to taste a spot on his neck and he was suddenly terrified he was going to come before he even got out of his fucking pants.

'Can we go in your apartment?'

He didn't answer. Just encircled her in his arms and took three big steps back and kicked the door shut.

Chapter Four

NO THINKING. SHE COULDN'T think. He'd surprised her and then she'd been lost in those eyes and wondering what his dark hair would feel like under her fingertips. What other parts of him would feel like under her fingertips. Casey didn't want to think. She thought all fucking day, every day. She thought well into the night. She thought about when would be a good time to move on. What people would think of her. If she should or if she could or if she wanted to.

And standing there, watching his mouth and the way he stood, how his body managed to be supremely relaxed and yet alert all at once, she had wanted him so fucking fiercely it had stolen her breath and she felt like she was panting.

It was in that moment that Casey decided. Maybe she'd regret it later, but maybe not. The only thing she cared about was the freeing feeling of acting on her urge. And her urge was to kiss Nick. To touch him and kiss him and feel his hands on her. Like in her dream.

So she'd done it. No thinking. She could think later.

'Look, I know your situation, and I don't want you to think that you have to–' He stopped talking when she tugged her sweater over her head. It was misty outside, only bordering on outright rain, and her hair and clothes were damp. She toed off her Vans and realised he was watching her.

'I know you know. And … can we not talk about that? Anything else. Say anything else to me,' she said, and unbuttoned her jeans.

His mouth worked for a moment but he didn't really

165

speak until she pushed her worn jeans over her hips, revealing small turquoise panties.

'I think you are possibly the most gorgeous woman I've ever seen,' he blurted.

Casey felt heat rise in her cheeks. 'Really? I mean …Christ, that sounded needy. It's just been a while is all.'

'Really.' He moved toward her slowly like she might spook.

Hell, for all Casey knew she might. But she did know this, Nick was the first guy who'd provoked any kind of lust or reaction or want from her in over a year. He was the first man who had made her think and dream and desire some kind of physical contact. And when she was still and quiet with herself, Casey realised she'd be a fool to let that go.

Even if she felt some sadness.

What was it that Annie always reminded her? And her own parents even, when they called from Michigan to check on her?

The sad just means you're human …

Casey swallowed hard and took a step in to meet him. His hand felt warm on her chilled skin as he swept it from her chest to her belly. The muscles tingled and jumped when he stroked her and she bit her lip. She felt like she might cry and hoped not, she wanted this to be liberating and sexy, not embarrassing and over emotional. And yet …

'You're in my head,' she confessed, feeling a little light headed.

He kissed her between the breasts – mouth soft and seeking as he licked at her skin like he was tasting her own personal flavour. His hands cradled her waist and he tugged her even closer so he could kiss her mouth. 'Am I? Hard to wrap my head around.'

'Yes, you are. And please, please don't pity me,' she said. There was a tiny little burst of emotion in her voice, it bordered on a sob and she heard it. Hated it.

166

'Hey,' he said, pushing her chin up so she had to meet his gaze. 'I don't pity you. I'm in awe of you. And I'm … grateful to you.'

Casey shook her head, fiercely, kissing him quiet, tugging his hair again as she pushed herself to him. His cock leapt at the small burst of pain she delivered and she smiled even as she felt like she might burst into tears. 'God, don't be super nice to me, please. You'll make me cry. And I don't want to cry. I want to–'

She shook her head.

Her panties slid lower as he pushed them, the seductive scrape of the soft cotton over her skin. The maddening heat of his palms on her. The way he cupped her ass. 'If you cry, you cry. I don't care. I just care that you want me. I just care that you think I'm good enough to–'

'Hush, hush!' she demanded and shoved him. Caught off guard Nick pin-wheeled and fell backward onto his caramel coloured sofa.

Casey kicked off her jeans, still looped around one ankle. Her panties followed and she swept her hair – crazy and messy and wavy from the rain – back off her forehead.

'I'm on the pill,' she whispered. 'And I'm safe and clean and–'

'Ditto. Well not the pill.'

He grinned and her heart cramped a little. God, he was pretty. And nice. And sexy as hell. A dangerous combo for a broken girl like her.

'I trust you.' She didn't know why she did. Or why she should. But something in her told her she could.

Casey didn't question herself as she yanked his jeans down. He had on grey boxer briefs and his cock was hard and pressed to his belly and she stalled for a minute just looking at him.

'Everything o–'

'Hush,' she said. She licked her lips, drinking him in. It was shocking to her what a visceral reaction she had to

167

seeing him. Bare and somewhat vulnerable and so fucking hot. 'Just hush,' she repeated, hooking her fingers in the waistband and tugging so he had to raise his hips to help her.

He was smooth and hard in her hand. They both sighed in unison and then laughed simultaneously too.

'We seem to be synched up,' Nick said, groaning just loud enough to make her grow wet and soft between the legs. He thrust up gently – as if he couldn't quite help it – and she squeezed his cock to prompt him to make that noise again.

Casey nodded, not trusting her voice. She was still afraid of crying – but mostly because she felt overwhelmed. Joy, fear, sadness, excitement – all of it swirled in her belly like a storm and she sighed, shimmying up over him, straddling him as he watched her with those stark blue eyes.

'My God, you're beautiful,' he said.

'Hush,' she repeated. 'Don't make me cry.'

He cupped her breasts and just held her that way, letting the heat of his hands cover the slight chill of her skin. Casey's nipples pebbled and the roughness of his palms made her shake a little.

'It's OK if you cry, though. I know–'

'I know you know.' She smiled. 'But don't actively try to make me.'

'I would never …'

But his words died on his lips as she trailed the tip of him along her labia. Nudging her clit with the helmet of his cock, she tried to keep her heart rate below the heart attack zone. The smell of him – all man and cotton and cosy heat on a chilly night – flooded her senses and Casey ran him over the soaking split of her pussy.

'That is making me … nuts.' He finished with a groan that set her nerves clanging in an entirely good way.

When she sank down on him, she watched him bite his lip.

'Tell me,' Casey said, knowing he was holding

something back.

'You feel just so ...'

'Wet?' She rocked down onto him, feeling that sweet invasive stretch of penetration.

'Yes, but–'

'Ready?' she sighed, rolling her hips to feel the press and stroke of him everywhere. Everywhere she needed it. Everywhere she *had* needed it for so long now.

'Tight,' he growled and thrust up under her, hard. The quick movement and the sudden roughness set her off and Casey came with a low moan that almost sounded like sadness but was soaked in joy and surrender.

She had done it. She'd come and it was good and he was good and ...

Her mind went blank when he pulled her down over his chest for a kiss. The fall of her hair shielding them both for a moment. His lips brushed hers and his tongue tangled with hers and then he nipped her, driving up from under her once more.

'Casey?'

'Yeah?'

'Do it again,' Nick said. Big hands clamped her hips, steadying her as he began to thrust into her from beneath. Now that he was doing it in earnest, she felt the head of his cock manipulating every single bundle of nerves that craved stimulation. Her G-spot seemed to bloom with heat and a slow flexing spasm began deep inside her.

Her fingers curled against the heat of him. She let herself be swept away, driving her body down to meet his thrusts. Welcoming his cock with the way she let her legs fall open just a tiny bit more.

'I'm–' She was going to tell him she was coming but he kissed her into silence, his tongue gently brutal against hers.

He held her as close as he could and filled her and her body rippled and then clamped down on him with the pleasure of it all. It stole her breath – the force of it – and

169

how he held her. Like he feared she might float off and away from him forever if he didn't.

His fingers whispered back and forth along her lower back as Nick thrust up once, twice, three times more and came with a low growl that made her shiver all over. The sound of a man losing his firm grasp on control. The sound of a man coming undone.

For her.

Oh God, it had been so long.

And then, even though somewhere in herself she expected it, they came. Dominating her senses, making her eyes water and her throat grow tight. Taking the air from her lungs and the sound from the room – all but the pounding of her heart.

The tears.

Casey tried to curl in on herself. She tried to roll into a protective ball and just ride them out. But Nick was having none of that. He held her firmly against himself, wrapped his arms around her, kissed her hair.

'Go ahead and cry, Casey. It's OK.'

'It's not–'

'It is. I'm not going anywhere. Hey, I knew your story from day one – well, today is day one. So, from moment one. From the moment you gave me a hard-on with nothing but your big toe.'

She snorted at that – unladylike – but a genuine laugh nonetheless. 'I don't want you to think that–'

'All I think is that you're having a lot of emotions right now. And I'm lucky enough to be here to hold you.'

That brought more stupid tears and she was torn between feeling affection, gratitude and annoyance. How does a person ruin such an awesome bout of sex with a bunch of embarrassing tears? She shook her head but let him hold her. She was lulled by the pound of his heart and the heat of his body and the way Nick kept sweeping his thumb along her skin as she clung to him.

170

She almost fell asleep. Almost.

But her phone started to beep and rattle in the depths of her jeans and she realised what she'd done.

'Oh, shit. That'll be Annie.'

WHERE R U? I HOPE A SERIAL KILLER DOESN'T HAV U.

Casey shook her head and tried to text with trembling fingers.

'Don't go,' Nick said from behind her. 'Let me get us something to drink. Wine? Beer? Tea?'

She almost said tea but said softly, 'Wine, please. I think I need it.'

'Was I that bad?' he asked, cocking an eyebrow and grinning at her. His cool water gaze made her feel naked even though he'd given her his button down shirt from the back of a nearby chair.

'No, I was.'

Nick suddenly leaned forward over the back of the sofa, surprising her into a gasp. 'You were far from bad, Casey. You were amazing and lovely and despite what you think ….' He shook his head as if gathering his words. 'Despite what you think, nothing you did was off-putting. I would be surprised if after all this time you didn't have a reaction.'

'You deal in nostalgia,' she whispered. Her text to Annie was momentarily forgotten.

'I do. And I know how powerful and important memories can be.' He stroked her chin for a split second and when she realised her throat ached too much to answer him, she simply nodded.

'I'll get our wine. Red or white? Sorry I'm not evolved enough to also offer blush.'

She snorted, genuinely amused and beyond grateful that he didn't think her an overemotional wreck. 'I hate blush.

Red all the way.'

'Ah, there's my girl,' he said with real affection.

She was grateful that he walked out before she started leaking again. Because the moment he cleared the kitchen doorway, a fresh sluice of tears were unleashed.

Chapter Five

IM W/NICK. SORRY. MAY NOT BE COMING.

Casey picked her cuticle and then forced herself to stop
before she bled. She held her breath as she waited for the
phone's patented chime. When it came she read:

WELL IF UR WITH NICK, YOU'D BETTER COME ;)

That made her laugh. Casey wondered how much of this
was Annie and how much of it was fate. Had her friend
asked this gorgeous, obviously kind, man to take pity on
her? Was she a pity fuck?

NO WORRIES ABOUT THAT. I DID. TWICE. BUT I
FEEL AWFUL.

Her vision doubled and then trebled and she wiped her
leaking eyes. Listening to Nick in the kitchen getting their
drinks had the lazy domestic sounds she missed so much.
The sound of another person in the house, moving around,
tinkering, making small noises. Not being alone – how much
had she craved the sound of another body on slow quiet
Sunday mornings?

Her phone burbled again and she read:

DONT. NICK IS A GOOD GUY. NICE. SWEET. HOT AS
HELL! IT'S TIME 4U TO DO THIS. NO GUILT!

She typed Kk, their signature sign off meaning *OK–OK!* and shut the phone. She would go home and process this. Casey needed to figure out if this was a favour to her friend or a pity fuck or … what.

He came in and she started, dropping the phone at her feet.

'Sorry,' he said. 'I didn't mean to–'

There was a knock at the door and they both turned. Her first thought was Annie but then he said, 'Damn. That must be my Chinese. Only a half hour or so late. Hungry?'

'No. Um … you get the door,' she said, taking the glasses he passed off.

Casey set them on the table and started to frantically shove her legs in her panties and jeans. She needed to get dressed and get out of here. She couldn't seem to breathe. Not at all.

She shut her eyes and sucked in a breath, forcing herself to hold it for a count of four before blowing it out. A trick the grief counsellor had taught her after Brendan died. It regulated your heart, gave you a boost of some chemical she couldn't remember and basically calmed you down.

When he came back with a bag of food, smiling like he loved the fact that she was here, her heart nearly broke.

'Hey, thanks but I … I have to go. I just remembered …' She shook her heard. What? What had she just remembered? That she couldn't handle this. That she'd left the gas on. That she was on the verge of crying again and was mortified by it. '… that I have to go,' she finished weakly.

'Casey–' he started.

'It's fine! It's good! Thanks so much for the um …' she wiggled her finger at the sofa. What? The sex? The orgasms? The fucking.

She was really bad at this.

'I'm sorry,' she said, hearing the emotion amping up in her voice and hating it. 'I just really have to go.'

She grabbed her phone from the floor and her purse and rushed past him before he could touch her. If he touched her, she would crumble. Casey was sure of it.

'Casey!' he called out after her as she headed for the stairwell. No time for the elevator. 'It's *OK!*'

She didn't stop. She hit the metal bar going full speed and started taking the steps as fast as she could.

Nick put the bag down, suddenly not hungry. He didn't know what to do. Stop her or not stop her. This wasn't just some fickle thing – this was a woman recovering from loss and he didn't want to push her.

Annie had filled him in just enough to know that what Casey had had with her late husband had been a bit of a fairy tale love. And he didn't want to disrespect her memories or feelings by rushing after her like they were in some romance movie.

He rummaged through the paperwork for the charity auction on the breakfast bar. Casey's number was printed at the top along with: *"Please call or text with any questions."*

He dialled, knowing in his gut she wasn't going to answer, but having to do this anyway. It had been ages since he'd been moved by a woman. Not just the way she looked, but by the way she acted, talked, smelled, laughed.

He'd seen something in her shyly horrified and yet bold expression when she'd hurt her ankle and inadvertently aroused him.

That was a woman he wanted to be around. To get to know.

And the feel and smell and remembrance of being inside of her, feeling her come, was enough to make his fingers stiff and clumsy as he dialled.

When her message came on – he knew she wouldn't answer – he momentarily froze. Forgetting everything he was going to say and then some.

Finally, fearing the message would click off leaving her

only with silence, he said, 'Hey … .listen. I'm sorry if I … did anything to make you feel bad. I loved being with you. I want to be with you more. Even just, you know, talking …'He chuckled softly, feeling like a pervert and a mental patient. He was sure he sounded like a horse's ass. 'But the other stuff was awesome …'

Nick blew out a sigh, fighting the urge to beat his head on the nearest wall. This was not playing out well. His mouth and brain seemed to be disconnected.

'Look, I sound like a moron. My point is. I was thrilled to see you today, and I was more than thrilled at the turn it took when you came in. And God … Casey, you are amazing. But it doesn't have to be about sex, you can just come talk to me. Or we can go hiking or get a drink or whatever you like to do. What I'm trying and failing to say is that I–'

'To hear your message, press seven. To erase your message, press four. To save and send your message press two or hang up.'

He hung up. Hopefully he didn't sound like a total dick.

She couldn't answer it. She just knew it was Nick and she was too embarrassed to talk to him. She'd shown up after a very dirty dream about him, attacked him, made him get naked and then burst into tears and ran away.
Every man's dream date, she was sure.

She'd blubbered and sniffled all the way home and now she found herself standing in her walk-in closet looking for something comforting to wear. She was chilled to the bone but found, embarrassingly, that she didn't want to take a shower. She wanted him to stay on her. The smell of him the feel of him and the remainder of him left inside of her.

Casey blushed when she realised it but shrugged. Fuck it. She had acted like a fool, but as for right now, she wanted to keep the essence of Nick on her. She wanted the smell of him to comfort her. She was not ashamed of being with him; she was ashamed of her reaction.

There were her favourite fleece pants peeking off the top shelf and a sweatshirt that had once been her dad's but she'd liberated it from him when she was 20. The thing was at least 15 years old. Standing on tiptoe, Casey yanked the pants and everything shifted, dumping a pile of clothes on top of her. A box fell off the shelf too, to land noisily at her feet.

'Jesus,' she sighed. Somewhere in her, though, she was grateful for the mess. It would give her time before having to listen to his message. But when Casey saw what was in the box, she changed her mind. A whole stack of mementos and photographs were stuffed inside and on the top of the pile was the last birthday card Brendan had given her. It had drifted open during the tumble and the line that rose up to smack her in the face read:

Casey, all I ever want for you in life is for you to always be happy ...

She waited. And waited. But no tears came.

'Of course not. Now that you're home alone and no one can see you or hear you, you are perfectly calm and in control.' She shook her head.

Putting all the stuff back in the box and placing it on the shelf with trembling hands, she drew out the clean up process. When she turned off the closet light she said, 'I miss you,' and headed to her bed.

It was chilly in her room and she bundled herself up, sipping from a bottle of water she always kept on her nightstand. The mist had turned to rain and Casey listened to it tapping against the windows. She played Nick's message back on speakerphone.

Her heart clamping tight, her stomach buzzing with nerves, her throat growing tight all over again. She shut her eyes and listened to his warm rich voice and when it ended, she was so touched and somewhat turned on by hearing him, she played it again.

She waited to cry, all over again. And didn't.

177

'No. Of course not,' she said yawning. 'You'll see him tomorrow. That's when you'll cry. No use crying if you can't make an ass of yourself, right?'

She snorted, softly and felt herself drifting. Good. She wanted to sleep. For a year now, sleep had been the only place she felt calm and in control. Being utterly unconscious had been her only source of true solace since losing Brendan.

When she woke her body was tangled in damp clothes. The sky was a gunmetal grey, spitting flecks of rain against her window.

Casey felt the thump and thrill in her pussy from her dream. She'd dreamt of his head between her legs. His fingers in her cunt. And then finally him, pinning her to the cool white wall of her bedroom, thrusting up and into her. Bringing her to that sound that only erupted from her when she was coming undone inside. When she surrendered to her pleasure.

'Jesus.' Casey ran a shaky hand through her hair. She couldn't quite shake the dream. She couldn't quite shake the images that skittered through her mind at top speed – her own personal porn movie.

And to think I only have to see him and act sane in a few short hours ...

There was no way. Casey rolled on her belly. Remembering the feel of him the night before. Remembering his length and his heat and his rigidity. Remembering how he held her, understood her, and ...

She shook her head. 'Pity fuck. Don't get too attached. No matter how you feel. Remember, you haven't felt *anything* in quite a while.'

But her body was excited; a wet pleasure-seeking pulse had started in her centre. Casey fumbled for her middle nightstand drawer and tugged it open. She removed a purple vibrator with a bulbous head and the perfect number two

178

setting – in Casey's personal opinion – it was her go-to-orgasm tool. If she had an orgasm now, maybe she'd be able to focus later.

Probably not. Not if Nick's there ...

But she had to try.

'Take one for the team,' she snickered and worked the fat broad tip over her slit to get it moist. When she set the buzzing plastic to her clitoris a warm spasm worked through her. Her pussy flexed and her stomach went light and buzzy.

It wasn't hard at all to get herself there. This is what happened when a man was just too good-looking to handle. When the thought of his hands on you made your mind go white with lust. This is what happened, Casey thought, pushing the now-slick toy inside her body.

Her channel spasmed greedily around the buzzing shaft as she called up her dream. His mouth on her mouth, her throat, her earlobes. How he'd teased each nipple into an erect peak of hard flesh.

Casey pinched her nipple with her free hand. When an echo of pleasure coursed through her, she pinched again, harder. Almost clamping her fingernails tight to her pink flesh.

She thumbed the vibrator from the tentative but nice setting of one, to the perfect pressure and vibration of level two.

'He was licking you,' she said to herself, pulling the toy free, running it over her engorged clit. Letting the vibration rumble through her entire pout. Outer lips and juicy folds and then her clit once more before driving it deep and tilting her hips to beat it against her G-spot.

'He was licking you and when he got you off, licking you ...' Her voice had come down to smoke and wind and a dry sound that reminded her of leaves on asphalt. 'When he got you off, he went for penetration. He slid into you. His big, hard cock forcing into your wet depths and ...'

She was talking dirty to herself. How insane was that?

179

But it didn't matter because her heartbeat had gone wild and her mind had narrowed down to nothing but the bright yellow intention of orgasm.

The toy banged her G-spot gently and she applied a tiny bit more pressure. 'He fucked you. Against the wall. He *took* you against the wall. He took you and he fucked you and ...'

The first lazy flex of orgasm worked through her and she bit her lip to keep her heart in her chest, because it felt as if it would leap free. 'And when you came,' she sighed, coming. Long, lazy, wet spasms deep in her cunt. They seemed to bleed warmly into her pelvis and her belly. Even her fingers felt heavy and lethargic. 'When you came, he ate every bit of juice you made with little wet flicks of his tongue on your pussy.'

And then she shut up, giving over to the forceful presence of her pleasure. She rode it to the peak and all the way back down. It left her feeling sleepy and relaxed and for a few minutes, Casey let herself lie there in bed, bathed in grey light. Listening to the gentle tap of water on the window. And for the last split second before climbing out of bed, she let herself imagine that if she turned to her side, she'd see him there. Nick, lying on his side watching her. Touching her hair. Kissing her lips. Smiling.

'What happened last night?' Annie was scurrying along the long hotel hallway to keep up with her.

'What, you mean you don't know? You mean he didn't fill you in?' She didn't mean for her voice to sound so hard and upset.

Annie stomped her foot and grabbed Casey's arm, halting her. Casey had a good nine inches on Annie's five feet, but Annie had a grip, especially when pissed.

'What is *wrong* with you?'

'You know I can totally get my own men. You know I can do it, don't you? You don't have to set me up with pity fu– dates.' Casey swallowed and swallowed again, willing herself not to cry. What was wrong with her? She didn't really mean what she was saying. Not really.

Annie clamped her mouth down tight and yanked Casey to one of the small alcoves along the hall set up for phone conversations. She turned quickly and literally pushed Casey into an upholstered red chair. 'What is going on with you? Have you gone mental?'

'No, I–' Casey shook her head.

'He was not a pity fuck,' her best friend hissed. 'He wasn't even supposed to be a fuck. He's a nice guy, in my building, not too hard to look at, a good heart and he said yes. Did you or did you not employ me to find you a bachelor?'

'I did,' Casey said. Her face was colouring, she could feel it and knew that should she look in one of the hotel's gilt-framed mirrors she'd see lobster red cheeks under her wind-wisped hair.

'So that is what I did. And *you* felt something. And *you* made a pit stop on your way to my place. And *you,* my darling fucked him,' Annie growled. But thank God she was keeping her voice low.

Startling Casey, she dropped to her knees, her bright blue full skirt swirling around her dainty legs. 'And good for you, honey! Good for you! But don't twist it all up in your head. I didn't set that man up to be anything other than a pretty face for charity. And you feel something for him. I can see it on your face.'

Casey shook her head, blinked away some tears, but she couldn't quite manage to refute what her friend was saying.

'And as irrational and maybe even crazy as that is – go for it! Don't run from it. Sweetie ...' Annie patted her knee and sighed. 'You deserve it. Let yourself be happy for God's sake. It might not go anywhere, but at least it'll be a step in the right direction.'

Saved by the hunks. She saw three of her men file past down the hall. Nick came along a few minutes later, a garment bag slung over his arm. She imagined him naked and smiling and feared she might pass out because she couldn't get any air.

He glanced their way and waved. It was a tentative shy wave but his smile warmed her.

'Did you hear me?' Annie demanded.

'Yes.'

'Will you stop this nonsense?'

'I'll try,' she said.

And she would. Casey promised herself that much.

Chapter Six

'OK, GENTLEMAN!' SHE MANAGED. Her voice cracked just a wee bit and Casey tried not to let it rile her. Her gaze ricocheted around, making her feel damn near dizzy, as she tried to look at anyone, *anything* but Nick.

But it was useless and when her gaze settled on his, he looked concerned and still sleepy and yes, sexy as hell. She sighed without meaning to and he cocked his head, giving her a little half smile that said they had a shared secret.

A shared, sensual, naughty … *naked* secret.

'Careful, your cheeks are so red I think I might need to go get a fire extinguisher,' Annie said out the side of her mouth. Her lips barely moved and somehow she managed to laugh without her face moving.

'We're going to do a final run-through. We'll go and then the other ladies' teams will go and then when that's happened we'll do a walk-through extravaganza!' She tried to smile and it felt like her face was going to split.

His eyes were on her. She could *feel* his gaze and it was wonderful and terrible at the same time. Casey was afraid she wouldn't be able to think at all with Nick in the room.

Her eyes settled on him again and he grinned. That grin went straight through her from the top of her head, zinging a trail through her gut, her girly bits and down to her toes. She cleared her throat. 'We're only going to do the patter – which will be talking you up, your stats and all that jazz – for the final run-through. Those things are often abs–' Her tongue stalled out and Casey heard her best friend snicker as if from a long distance away.

She clenched her ass to keep herself from passing out, a trick an ex boyfriend who flew fighter planes had taught her. Nick looked amused, too and Casey forced herself to rush on. Even with the flickering image of him thrusting up hard from beneath her. Even when she remembered that shared explosive moment of release.

She shook her head. 'Ad-libbed, is what I meant to say,' she barrelled on. 'We'll just sort of wing it while making sure to give your appropriate info. Height, job, length–'

Damn.

Annie was damn near choking next to her, covering her mouth with her hand. But her shoulders were shaking and a few of the guys laughed too and Nick – well Nick blushed a lovely shade of tomato but smiled.

'Weight!' she barked.

Fuck-fuck-fuck.

'In this order please: Matthew; Sam; Robert; Bobby; Brian and Nick coming in the rear.'

Annie squawked and this time a full-blown ripple of laughter worked its way down the line. Even the other group of men who were near the far end of the room working with another leader were listening and laughing.

Casey, bit her tongue and tried to breathe. 'Bringing up the rear, coming up in the rear, whatever!' she said, and actually groaned. 'He will be last is what I'm trying to say and if everyone is done being in Kindergarten we can–'

'Easy,' Annie warned. 'They volunteered for this.'

'Would everyone please line up?' she chirped. 'Thank you.'

Annie started to say something and Casey shoved the clipboard at her. 'Start.'

Then she rushed into the coat room and put her forehead to the cool wall. Maybe she would save them all the embarrassment of the rest of the day and simply drop dead.

'Hey.'

Casey jumped but then his hands were on her and she

settled, going from spooked to calm in such a short amount of time it startled her. Nick wrapped his arms around her and nuzzled the back of her neck, the side of her face.

Casey shut her eyes, liking the feel of his embrace, the steady pound of his heart against her back, his breath in her hair. 'You OK?'

'You should be out there,' she said. But even as she said it she arched her bottom back against him. She felt the first tentative stirring of his cock. Her mind's eye showed her Nick flipping her skirt up, yanking her panties to the side and slamming his co–

'I'm coming up in the rear,' he chuckled and pressed himself against her.

Casey's breath died in her lungs even as she started to laugh with him. She really did want him. Desperately. And beyond wanting him, she needed him. A troubling and yet honest urge to be with him had taken root in her gut and wouldn't release her.

'Can you please ...' She shook her head.

He bent his head a bit lower and said, 'Pardon?'

'Can you ... can we ... is the door locked?'

He moaned softly in her ear and his fingers slid a bit lower on her waist, the tips of his fingers grazing the top of her mound through her skirt and panties.

'It is locked. So we could talk without intrusion. Annie's out there getting everyone in line and fixing some stuff and –'

Casey cut him off by turning in the cage of his arms and grabbing his dark hair. She kissed him, her mouth open and needy, her fingers playing along his belt buckle trying to find the end of his belt so she could tug him free.

Nick's fingers warred with hers as she helped him and finally, lacking patience, Casey batted his hands away once he'd undone his button. She shoved her hand into his pants and found him long and hard and hot in her palm.

'I dreamed about you,' she frantically confessed.

185

'Was it dirty?' He kissed down her neck and nibbled the place where her pulse jumped beneath her skin.

'Filthy.'

'Did I–'

'You did it all,' she informed him and shoved, completely unladylike, she knew, his pants down around his knees.

'And …'

Casey pulled back and stared at him. His blue eyes were sweetly intrusive and he made her heart skip around erratically. She told him the truth while stroking his cock. 'I woke up and got myself off.'

'Turn around. Turn around,' he ordered. His face unreadable and starkly handsome in the coatroom's dim light.

She obeyed, feeling a thrill tumble in her belly and a heat unfurl in her cunt. He was going to take her. Just like in the dream. The world seemed to spin and Nick reached around her, slamming one of her hands and then the other to the cool painted cinderblock wall.

'Spread your legs,' he demanded.

She widened her stance even as he hiked her skirt up and groaned roughly when he saw her grey silk panties. His hands smoothed over the sinful fabric and Casey was aware of goose bumps blossoming along her thighs. He fingered the elastic leg bands and whispered, his lips pressed to her ear, 'I'd rip these things but I like them, Casey. And I'd like to see you in them again. When we can take our time. So for now …'

Nick shoved them down and she stayed there, panties keeping her lower legs about a hip width apart. It would work. It would work … she thought frantically. Casey titled her hips forward to present her ass and open herself to him. So he could slide into her.

So he can penetrate you …

She shivered joyfully at that dirty random thought.

And then he was running the balmy tip of his cock to her opening. Her pussy flexed eagerly. Nick pressed his mouth to her ear again and said, 'We have to hurry. But later, I won't want to hurry.'

She nodded, mindlessly, over and over again. His fingers dug into her waist and he thrust slowly, entering her inch by inch. Stretching her gorgeously so that she panted and chewed her bottom lip to keep herself quiet. She needed to be quiet. She needed to keep herself together.

Casey scratched her nails along the wall, pushing herself back every single time Nick thrust. Driving him deeper with her motion, getting him exactly where she needed him to be. He rumbled and it was the most amazing sound she'd heard in a long time. There was such a raw and animal quality to it that she felt a quiver crawl up her back.

His fingers pulled away from her only to be replaced by one big forearm looped around her waist. With his other hand he stroked her leg, her side, her ass almost restlessly before finally bringing it around to find her throbbing clit with his fingers.

'Come for me, Casey. Come for me and know it's OK, and Christ, don't run from me this time. You damn near broke my heart. Crazy just 24 hours in … but true.'

He grunted with raw need, his rhythm growing chaotic. His finger pinched and plucked and swirled until she had to bite her tongue so hard she saw stars because she was coming. Drawn-out damp contractions milking his cock so he slammed hard and high into her once more and came. Gripping her so tight around the middle she almost wheezed. Casey heard herself laughing softly as they peaked and her cunt continued to ripple around him until she felt like she was no more than warm blood and soft bone.

If not for her arms steadying them by bracing against the wall, she was almost sure they'd have dropped to the floor right there.

A tentative knock sounded and she had to steady her

breath before calling out, 'Yes?'

And she still sounded flighty and twittery.

'Um … we're ready for him. And you. We have been. I hope you're …' the words trailed off and then Annie snorted and mumbled, '*done'*.

'If I blush any harder, I'm going to burst into flames,' she told Nick. And then she pulled her knickers up.

He didn't say anything, just tugged the ends of her hair so she was forced to take a step toward him, her skirt drifting back down around her hips and then her knees.

'Don't run,' he whispered, kissing her. 'Don't run.'

Nick watched her as he waited for his turn. Twin spots of colour still decorated her pale cheeks and made the caramel coloured freckles on her nose stand out all the more. He had to shake off the thoughts now cavorting in his mind. How desperate she had sounded. Desperate for him, a realisation so startling it was like a punch in the face. How she'd bent to his will, presented herself, taken him with her willing backward thrusts. How she'd sounded as she tried to stifle her noises. Her fingernails whispering on the wall. The thick and prolonged spasms in that sweet pussy as she came.

He'd loved the way she kissed him before and the way she kissed him back after.

The smell of her still filled his nose and if he inhaled deeply, he could smell the mingled scent of them. He smelled like sex. Which meant she did too.

He caught her looking, her intelligent brown eyes still sparkling with leftover arousal and the glow of release. My God, how gorgeous could one woman be? Her hair was a wild perfect mess and he remembered it tickling his chin as she moved under him, her orgasm driving her clit against his fingers.

He lifted a finger to his face as she watched and smelled it. The scent of her was all over his skin. She blushed and smiled and looked away – but not for long. She looked back

188

quickly, biting her lip as she called out the next bachelor's name for him to walk.

Her nipples were hard buttons pressing up from beneath the thin material of her blouse. He could see them spiking the fabric and even with a bra on, they were so hard that his mind was suddenly full of the image of rolling them over his tongue before biting the tips.

You're going to give yourself a hard-on, genius ...

She finally called his name and Nick moved forward on feet that felt numb and heavy. He could hear her, stumbling over her words, cut at first but then what she was saying leaked into his head.

'Nick is an ... um ... he's a refurbisher. He's six foot three, one hundred and ninety-eight pounds with gorgeous blue eyes ...'

She blushed and he nearly stopped on the stupid runway. He felt like an idiot but he was doing it for a good cause as Annie had pounded into his head about a zillion times while trying to convince him to do it. How her friend was so awesome and really needed this and it would make her so happy and ...

'He deals in taking not so beautiful things and making them beautiful. In nostalgia.'

She smiled at him and his stomach dropped. The five other guys were much more accomplished than him. There was a doctor, a neurosurgeon, an attorney, a fireman and a dentist.

I redo furniture. Sometimes houses. Sometimes art ... but ...

He was going to let her down. There was no way he'd garner the kind of money these guys did. He felt like a horse's ass and it was all Nick could do to finish what he was supposed to do on stage and not flee the scene as it were.

He wanted to make her happy and he'd probably be lucky to earn enough for a dinner, let alone enough to make a difference to research.

He fisted his hands to keep him calm. He'd have to think it over. There had to be a way to make things right.

Chapter Seven

THE THOUGHT OF AUCTIONING him off to another woman, even for a night, was enough to make her see red.

'You need to get over that, you dingus.' Casey fit her key into the door.

It was just past three and she hadn't eaten all day. Annie and everyone else had eaten at the hotel and then Annie had headed off to her shift at the book store. Casey, once again, found herself grateful that Brendan's life insurance had left her in a position to do charity work for now. She wanted to work but wasn't sure at what just yet. This gave her time to think and be productive.

One of her dreams had always been to open an antique store or just a second hand store. When she pondered it, the Jiminy Cricket in her head said, *and then Nick can refurbish things for you and you can live happily ever af–*

'Shut it, Jiminy.'

She pulled a container of parmesan noodles from the fridge and put the leftovers in the toaster oven. She washed her hands and started making a small salad as her stomach growled angrily.

She'd have to auction him off. It was for charity, it wasn't like she was pimping him out for stud service. Casey snorted and rolled her eyes. 'You have gone mental,' she said.

She sat in front of the afternoon talk shows and ate her noodles and salad. Then she kicked off her heels and pulled off her thigh highs. Her body still thumped and quivered whenever she let herself remember him moving behind her, flipping her skirt up, fucking her as she pushed her hands to those rough cinderblocks.

Casey took a long hot shower and then dressed in leggings and thick wool socks. The fall weather was truly turning toward cold because the house read 67 degrees. Her favourite navy blue pullover swathed her in warm thick cotton from neck to mid thigh and she decided that a salted caramel hot chocolate was just what the chill weather ordered.

With whipped cream.

She'd taken her first salty-sweet sip when the doorbell rang. Casey hurried to answer. 'You're here!' she said, licking her lips.

'Annie gave me your address,' he muttered. His gaze was locked on her lips.

Nick leaned in and licked her upper lip with the tip of his tongue and her heart quickened. 'Sorry,' he whispered, running his thumb along her lower lip. 'You had something …'He licked his lips and looked intent. 'Whipped cream? It was on your lip.'

'It is whipped cream. I just made a hot chocolate. Want one?'

'Can I come in for it?'

She gasped and took a step back, letting a bit of the rain and a few dead leaves sweep in with him. 'Sorry – sorry. You turn my brain to mush, you know.' She said it to her wool socks. It was too big a statement to say it right to him.

'You pretty much do the same thing to me. And I'd love a hot chocolate.'

'Walk this way.' She led him to the kitchen and when Casey turned he was behind her mimicking her walk by swaying his hips like a woman. Lean hips shimmying and his upper body rotating and his stance a bit girlish.

Casey covered her mouth as hysterical laughter bubbled out of her. 'Oh God.'

'You said, walk this way.' He grinned and she felt the

urge to smash herself up against him and kiss him until their clothes fell off.

Casey turned from him, rattled by her urgent need to touch and kiss him. She set the water on to boil and measured out the dark cocoa, the sea salt, a few squirts of caramel. She added a touch of cream to give it that really decadent richness and waited for the water.

'Are you OK with the auction? You often look like you want to run away.' She wanted him to feel comfortable and here was as good a chance as any to let him off the hook.

'Well,' he sighed, seating himself on one of the high stools. 'I came here to ask you a favour.'

'What's that?'

'Will you bid on me if no one does?'

'What do you mean if no one does?' she asked, laughing. Casey could hear the water starting to jump and simmer in the pot.

'I'm not ... I'm not like the other guys. I'm a restorer, basically. I work with furniture and fabric and upholstery. Some people would call it junk.'

'Well those people are morons.' She mixed her concoction put his drink in front of him. Steam curled and danced around his face.

'I just want to make sure we save face.'

'You will be bid on, Nick,' she assured him. Casey allowed herself to stroke her fingernail along his knuckles, one at a time. The colour came up in his cheeks and he shifted just a bit in his seat. 'I promise,' she said.

He ran his fingers over the lip of the counter and Casey tried not to be distracted by it. 'Mmm,' he said, licking his lips. 'Good stuff.'

'The trick is the salt. Are you sure you're OK? I thought I was the only one freaking out.' Her fingers tickled a bit higher, stroking his wrist and then up under the cuff of his blue button down.

Nick reached into his back pocket and tossed an envelope

on the counter. 'There's the money.'

'Money? What money?' For a split second she thought he was offering her money for sex. And she almost hit him. Hard. But then he shook his head looking as worried as ever.

'The money for me. The money to bid on me so I'm not the dud.'

'Dud, my ass,' she said, pushing the money back. 'You're the hottest guy there.'

'That's because you slept with me. You have to think that.'

'Nonsense.' She went around to hug him and when she got close, that magnetic pull he had on her became overwhelming.

'I'm the filler. I'm the bread crumbs in the crab cake,' he laughed, running a strong, nicked-up hand through his thick short hair.

'I'm the pity fuck,' she blurted.

Nick's eyes flashed, icy and assessing. 'What? What the hell are you talking about?'

She swallowed hard; here came all those pesky fucking emotions. 'Annie asked you to ... and you ... and we ...' She shook her head. That had been effective. 'I'm the pity fuck,' she repeated as if that explained it all.

'You're no such thing.' He grabbed her wrist, squeezing it hard enough to grind the fine bones and make her wince. But there was also a sparkle-flare of arousal under the lancet of pain.

'Are you sure?' she sighed, feeling suddenly exhausted. 'Because it's OK if I am.'

'No, it's not.' He looked pissed. 'And the fact that you would think that makes me feel like I haven't really explained to you what I think of you.'

'You have but–'

'I think you're amazing.' He ran his finger over the purplish blue veins on the inside of her wrist. Then he tugged her forward so he could kiss her. 'I think you're sexy

194

and sweet and funny and smart and you obviously have a big heart.'

'And a dead husband, hence the pity fuck.'

'Casey!' he said, shaking her.

'I'm just saying ... Hey!' She let him yank her gently into his lap and there, waiting for her after their shared kiss, was the hard hump of his erection beneath her ass. 'You're the one who's worried you won't get bid on.'

'So maybe we both need to work on our self esteem. What do you want to do, Casey?'

'Fuck you,' she said, the words tearing free of her lips before she could think about it.

Nick groaned. He took her face in his hands, his fingers sweeping along her cheekbones. When he kissed her, he nipped her lower lip so she startled and sighed. 'I meant with your life,' he said.

'I like the charity stuff,' she muttered, unbuckling his belt. 'But I really like antiques, used treasures, I'd like a store, I think.'

He kissed her again, sliding his slick tongue inside her mouth, making her breath shake in her lungs. 'Are you messing with me?'

'No, why?' She curled her fingers around him, rubbing her thumb over the slit at the tip of him. A small jewel of pre-come lubricated her skin over his and he groaned a second time.

'Because it sounds so much like what I ...' He shook his head, letting his eyes drift shut. Lost in her touch and what they were doing.

'Now bear with me,' she whispered against his jaw before kissing him once more. 'It's been a long time since I've done this.'

Casey dropped to her knees between his splayed thighs. His jeans were open, his cock out. She nuzzled her cheek to the warmth of his flesh. Her tongue darted out to gather the sweet and salty dot of fluid on his skin. She sucked the head

195

of his cock into her mouth and licked him, keeping her eyes on his face. The look he got, the way his jaw clenched and his eyes kept drifting shut only for him to wrench them open. Amazing.

'I don't think you've forgotten anything.' Nick put his hand on the back of her head, gently pushing her just enough that she was forced to take him deeper into her throat.

She sucked him hard, tasting the soap and sweat and cotton on his skin. His other hand joined the fray and she got a jolt of electricity low in her gut when she felt him thrusting up under her. He'd lost his firm grasp on manners and mores and was fucking her mouth.

Casey stroked his balls with her fingertips curled against that paper-thin skin. Nick shifted just enough to give her better access and she took that moment to draw the firm tip of her tongue along the blushing blue veins of his cock. She licked hard against the small gaping slit at the top of his erection and then swallowed him down.

She was mildly confused when he pushed her back, pulling free of her mouth, shoving her back only to yank down her leggings and wrestle her socks. He turned, shoved, lifted and she found herself airborne, hair flying, gasping.

Casey's ass hit the counter and he said, 'I'll clean your counter, I swear. I swear. Clean, clean,' he repeated like mantra and then he dropped to his knees between her legs, spread her wide with rough hands and latched his mouth to her slick cunt.

'Oh,' she said like it was all a big surprise.

It only took him a few good licks, a flat brandishing of his heated tongue to her clit and the plump labia that framed it. On the final drag of his tongue over her, she came, fingers gripping the cool edge of the counter to steady herself.

He stood fast – his movement urgent – and positioned himself at her opening. Keeping his eyes on her face, he slid into her with a lazy kind of reserve. She could tell by the dancing bunching muscles at his jaw that it was taking all his strength to keep his body calm and slow.

'Keeping yourself on a tight leash?' Casey whispered. She pressed her palms to his strong chest, feeling the gallop of his heartbeat under her hand. 'I wish this was gone. I wish I could feel your skin.'

He ripped the button down over his head without using the buttons. The white tee he wore underneath, that simply said MARYLAND WINE FESTIVAL, went sailing across the room next. And she was pushing the pads of her fingers and the palms of her hands to his quite alive, quite hot flesh.

He buried into her to his root, the soft slap of his balls against her ass, made her smile and she wrapped her legs around his waist to part herself even more for him. To open to him – get him deeper.

Nick claimed her mouth with his, his tongue brutal and insistent and sweet.

'Is this what you wanted,' he rasped, driving into her.

'Yes.'

'And you'll bid on me?'

'You'll get bid on,' she said, her voice turning wispy as she got closer to orgasm.

'*You'll* bid on me,' he repeated. He thrust deep and very unexpectedly pinched her ass cheek so her cunt clenched tight around him with adrenaline and surprise.

She nodded stupidly, fighting the rising orgasm. She didn't want to come yet. 'Yes, I'll bid on you. I will. I promise. If you …'

She broke off there, because he'd leaned back just enough to watch his cock sliding in and out of her. He watched attentively as her body ate his up an inch at a time and then let him go when he withdrew. His thumb pressed the thumping knot of her clit and he applied pressure and slow circles until she was panting, hooking her ankles behind his hips and letting her head fall back as she came. The overhead kitchen lights spurring sparkles and shimmers in her eyes.

A fine tremor had started in her entire body and he sprawled over her, sucked her nipple hard enough to make her heart skip. 'Come for me again. God, I love to watch you come. You look so … untamed when you come.

He gripped her hips tighter, losing his control – his rhythm growing as untamed as he claimed she looked. Casey pushed herself forward in short little burst to take him and when he growled, 'Fuck,' she knew he'd lost his control.

And that was what tipped her over the edge again. Him losing his steely strong tether to control.

She came with her arms wrapped around his neck, legs wrapped around his waist, body clamping and spasming around his as he emptied into her.

Casey pushed her lips to his neck, feeling his pulse thundering under her lips. She wondered if she bid enough if she could keep him. Just for a little while.

Chapter Eight

HE WANTED TO STAY but could tell that she got scared after. They'd stayed locked there in an embrace, her perched on the counter, him secured in her arms. It had felt perfect and right and wonderful. But in the end she had promised to bid on him if no one did. And that was what made him feel some relief in his gut.

'Now what are you going to do about the fact that you seem to be falling for her?' he asked himself, moving slowly around his apartment. Touching the sofa where they had been, imagining he could feel her there. Her energy.

Casey was beautiful and brilliant and kind. The mere fact that she was certain he'd earn as many bids as all the other bachelors spoke of her good heart. It had never occurred to her that he would be "less than" in some of the bidders' eyes because he basically lived a somewhat struggling but often artistic living. Sometimes he was flush; sometimes he ate noodles every night for dinner.

'She wants an antique store. Second hand,' he muttered.

He grabbed a beer from the fridge and tried to remind himself that she'd just lost her husband. Not much more than a year ago. And he had clearly been someone she loved very much. She probably wasn't ready for him, no matter how nice she thought he was.

Someone knocked and he had a ridiculous romantic moment imagining it was her. But when he put an eye to the peephole he saw Annie's smiling face.

'So ... how was ... did you? Jesus, have you actually asked her out yet or are you two doing this magnets drawn

199

to each other bullshit.'

'Why hi, Annie. Come on in,' he said, laughing as she barrelled past him.

She opened his fridge and grabbed a bottle of beer, twisting off the cap.

'Would you like a beer?' he asked, trying to keep a straight face.

'Don't hurt her,' Annie said, plopping down on his sofa.

'I wouldn't.'

'She's all fragile and dented. She doesn't think she is, but she is. But I see the way you look at her.' She pointed the neck of her beer bottle at him and winked. 'And, honey, I've seen her look at you. She's got it bad. You make her feel …' Annie rolled her hands around in the air searching for a word. Finally she shrugged. 'Feel *stuff,* I guess. I haven't seen that much colour in her cheeks since Brendan. Now don't fuck it up.'

'Christ, Annie. No pressure there!' Nick drained his beer, remembering the taste of Casey. It was still on his skin. He could smell Casey and the scent of their coupling and it was making him insane.

She waved her bottle at him. 'Cheers. You'll do fine. Tomorrow's the big auction and then you can get down to the business of courting her. And not just banging her in the coatroom.' She winked at him.

Nick shook his head. 'Just for the record, that was her idea.'

'I'm sure it was, cowboy.' Annie left quickly and he felt more confused than when she'd come.

Nick took a shower and did the only thing a man could do when the smell of a woman he was currently falling for was all over him. He stood in the hot spray, stroking his cock, replaying it all in his mind. The fragrant pink knot of her clitoris under his tongue. The petal pink of her outer lips that bled to rose red in the centre. The blushing wet invitation of her cunt. Christ, the way it felt to slide into her, inch by impatient inch, until he was buried in her, balls deep. And the way she kissed him.

Fuck, the way she kissed him.

He came with a long slow exhalation. Hoping he didn't fuck this up. Hoping he could make her proud and hoping, more than anything, that she'd give him a real chance when all was said and done.

She was going to throw up. She was. It was almost a done deal. Casey nervously twirled a lock of her hair around her finger. She shuffled and reshuffled her papers over and over again with her notes. She was having a heart attack. She was not going to make it. The other groups of bachelors were going first and she was the grand finale.

'You're not going to throw up and you're not having a heart attack.' Annie waltzed up and handed her a coffee.

Casey couldn't help but wonder how morning had come so fast. It seemed like mere minutes ago that she'd been doing very bad things in her kitchen with Nick.

'Stop reading my mind.'

'Has your new beau shown up yet?'

'He's not my beau,' Casey sighed, sipping her coffee.

'Fuck buddy?' Annie asked, cocking her head.

'Annie!' Casey shook her head.

'Well, you're smitten, and won't admit it, he's already hopeless over you and you're banging like bunnies, but you won't claim him as your beau so …'

'OK, so I'm attracted to him.'

'Wow. Really? What a news flash.' Annie laughed and then, 'Oh look. Speak of the devil and he shall appear.'

He looked sexy as hell. His dark hair was still damp and his blue eyes were drawn right to her. Casey felt that lightning stab of attraction that always came with seeing him. 'Hi,' she mouthed.

He smiled at her and echoed her "hi". Her mind was flooded with X-rated images of them at her counter. How they'd sipped their coffee after and he'd made her laugh by disinfecting the whole countertop. And then he'd explained how his business fluctuated. She'd asked him where the money had come from and Nick had copped to just wrapping up a heavy duty refurbishing for a local Catholic church.

The money was in her purse but she knew she wouldn't need to use it. The women would eat him up.

'Excuse me,' she said to Annie and hurried into the coat room.

She couldn't breathe. She wasn't going to throw up or have a heart attack. She was going to faint. She leaned against the wall, shut her eyes and forced herself to breathe.

'You OK?'

She jumped a little, clutching her heart. 'No. I feel like … I'm being electrocuted. I just … why?' she asked suddenly. She needed to know why this man – this handsome gorgeous sweet man – was not with someone. He had to be picky. And if he was, she was too broken and useless for the likes of him.

'Why what?' He leaned against her and pinned her to the wall. The kiss he laid on her was sexy and sweet and it made her want to lock the door and redo everything they'd done the night before.

'Why are you not with someone?' she asked, breathless.

Nick pulled back to look her in the eye. 'No real reason. No big story. Nothing earth-shattering, or brilliant or tragic. No "movie of the week" reason,' he said, pressing his thumb to her bottom lip before kissing her again. An almost chaste but entirely mind-melting kiss. 'Just a long, long line of "meh" relationships that didn't give me any reason to look forward to another.'

'Oh,' she gasped. He'd pressed against her fully and Casey could smell his soap and that shampoo in his hair. It smelled like sweet almonds.

'Until you.'

'Me?'

'You. You're … you. You are so … *you*. I just …' He shook his head. 'I sound like an idiot, but I just feel drawn to you, Casey. And being with you, being in you, just talking to you … it makes me nuts.'

Someone knocked. 'We are almost ready to begin,' one of the other organisers called loudly.

'I imagine I can hear the frown and disapproval in her voice,' Casey snickered.

'I can hear it too. Now listen. Don't leave me hanging. Bid on me and the money I gave you can go to this good cause of yours. No worries.'

'You will *not* need me to,' she said again. She felt suddenly frantic to make him understand. She grabbed Nick by the shoulders and held him tight. 'You're a good man. You're funny and sexy and kind. You are completely hot and um … in bed, might I just say *wow*. And you're …' She shook her head, feeling impotent in the explanation department. 'You are also very much you. And worth a ton of bids.'

Another brisk knock and they both shouted, 'Coming!'

Then he kissed her once more, his tongue gently brutish on hers. Joking, he growled in her ear, 'God, I really wish we were coming.'

'Soon,' she said. 'Because I wish it too.'

Pulling her from the wall and embracing her from behind, he pressed his mouth to her ear and wrapped his arms around her tighter. When he cupped her breasts and said hotly, 'Ooh, dirty talk,' her nipples spiked.

Another knock.

'I. Am. Coming!' she yelled and he laughed. Casey smoothed her hair. 'My God, what would my dead husband think?'

Nick went serious and said, 'How do you feel?'

'Nervous, excited … happy.' She said the last so softly it was barely a word.

Nick tilted her chin up and looked at her. 'I think that last one is the one he'd care about.'

'And for the record,' she said, kissing him quickly and hustling toward the locked door. 'He'd like you. He'd think you're a good man.'

She saw his throat work a little but then he smiled.

She took a deep breath. 'No time for that. Come on. Chop-chop. We need to sell your fine ass.'

The serious look fled and he followed her out, shaking his head and laughing.

At the door, Casey smiled at a very pinched-looking matron, named Marian Monroe. She nodded and winked. 'How goes it, Mad Marian?'

It was a secret name they all called Marian who had a bit of a dominatrix streak. They all wondered aloud, when she wasn't around, exactly what it was going to take to prompt her to show up with a whip and nipple clamps.

Another low chuckle from Nick, and Casey kept marching. It was time to do this thing. She was excited to earn money for the charity but equally excited to get the event over with. It had been a ton of stress and she was very ready for some quiet days by a cosy fire in some comfy clothes and some real nice wine and a very, very handsome man.

'Look, you're daydreaming domestication,' she muttered and took her place in line for the announcing. The room was now officially packed with women who could afford to do things like bid on handsome men to benefit ill people.

The fund raiser was underway and as was her way she was feeling calmer. Casey tended to freak out before the fact and find her Zen once the show was on.

She looked at Nick who winked and went to find Annie who had her purse. She wouldn't need the money but based on the look on his face – how adorable was it that he was so nervous –he wouldn't relax until he knew she had it.

The first presenter took the stage. Isabella Guy was the

picture of calm refinement as she announced her half dozen bachelors.

None of them are half as hot as Nick ...

Casey rolled her eyes at her own love-struck thoughts. She was so in over her head.

Chapter Nine

SHE DID OK UNTIL it was Nick's turn. Then her tongue sort of tangled up on itself and her brain went blank and Casey heard herself say, 'And this is Nick.' Only she nearly drew his name out as if in mid-orgasm. *Niii-ick.* She heard Annie snicker and was pretty sure, even from a distance, she saw Nick blush.

Oh my God.

'Nick is …'

What? Nick is what?

'Tall.'

Annie actually burbled then, like some wild jungle bird and Casey had a fleeting wish for a shotgun.

'And he is … um …'

Think!

'Big.'

Annie literally whooped.

Big! Oh God, you said big. Now you know everyone is thinking … penis!

'Not like that!' she amended loudly into the microphone.

That was when Annie had to leave the room.

Oh fuck. Now they all think he has a small cock...

'I mean, that, um … he's fine in the … oh, God.'

Most of the women in the room were staring at her as if she'd suddenly sprouted a second head and it was spewing vulgarities in French or possibly shouting out orders in Swedish. The overall look of the room was annoyed confusion.

'He's got blue eyes and dark hair and … walk!' she said

to Nick who had frozen at the steps of the stage as if unsure of what to do.

It was a disaster.

But he gave her a small amused smile that lit her up from the inside and started to walk.

'He's a refurbisher,' she said, having completely given up any hope of sounding in control of herself. 'So he deals a lot with nostalgia,' she said, remembering what he'd said. 'And he is very good with fragile things,' she added, her voice a little thick.

He stopped to look at her and she saw so much affection in that look her heart skittered sideways in her chest and actually stalled for a second.

'Like hearts and feelings,' she barrelled on, holding the microphone in a death grip.

His face softened and he started to come at her. She swallowed hard, shook her head, waved her finger as if to say, "walk".

'He's a very good kisser and ...'

Someone gasped and someone sighed and someone laughed. No one was bidding. Why? Why!

He looked concerned but not panicky. He was too busy listening to her.

'And he'd never ... ya know ... there is no pity. He's a genuine man,' she said softly. And then, 'One thousand dollars.'

It wouldn't be his money, this would be her own. This would be for the charity that would help save lives and to honour Brendan and to celebrate maybe a new start.

'Did I mention he's a good kisser and a good ... ?'

There was a pregnant pause in the entire room. She could feel it. Silence and attention crushing in on her like a silent, invisible weight. Nick had frozen in place on the runway and was watching her, eyes wide but full of humour, mouth a small "o" of surprise, huge handsome self in a holding pattern as she babbled.

'Good at, um ... other *stuff.* Two thousand. No, not two ... I'm remembering last night ...' She realised she'd said it aloud and her cheeks flooded with heat, but fuck it. 'So five thousand.'

In her peripheral vision she saw a woman start to lift her paddle and she turned, pointed and said, 'Don't even think about it, Angela.'

The woman promptly dropped her paddle and grinned. Casey said, 'Sold! To me. For five thousand dollars. Where's Annie?'

Annie poked her head in from the hallway and she said as calmly as she could manage into the microphone. 'And now my friend Annie – whose fault this is, FYI – is going to wrap up this program for you because I'm taking my bachelor to go.'

She put the microphone down and walked out to grab Nick's hand. But he grabbed her instead and bent her backwards, planting a movie-worthy kiss on her, right there.

'Hurry. Hurry, take me home,' she said. 'I need you.'

'Nicest thing a woman's said to me in years,' he whispered.

They didn't make it home. Her car was parked all the way in the back of the hotel parking-lot under a cluster of trees. They fell into the back seat tangled together.

'Thank God for tinted windows. Thank God for–'

He cut her off with a kiss, his body heavy over hers as he wrestled clumsily with her skirt.

'Those buttons are fake,' she squealed, laughing as she undid the back zipper herself.

'Silly women's clothes. Who needs fake buttons?' he growled.

Casey shimmied and shook and contorted and finally, tangled but ready, they were partially bare. And she kissed him, holding his head in her hands, toying her tongue along his. The feel of his cock, pressed hard and warm to the split of her pussy lips was maddening. But she wanted to be tortured just a little.

Casey thrust her hips up gently, rubbing her sex to his erection until he made a noise like an animal and roughly pinned her hips. And then it was Nick rubbing his hard-on to her labia. Every so often the pressure and mild friction on her clit made her hiss.

'I think I'm falling in love with you,' he said, stilling. 'When I saw you up there, so obviously sinking but so intent on … talking. And what you said about me–'

'Shh,' she pressed her finger to his lips. He kissed her finger and then sucked it into the soaking wet velvet of his mouth.

Her pussy clenched with arousal and butterflies buzzed in her stomach. She thrust her finger a bit deeper, barely able to make out his eyes in the shaded car. But he rocked against her, creating a fresh slide of fluid between her thighs.

She rotated her hips to let her legs fall open a bit. For him to feel her heat, her wetness – to tempt him.

And he sucked her finger again making her moan.

'It's how I feel. Do I have to hide it?'

'No,' she said, spreading them a bit more. 'Just be gentle with me, my heart, I mean. Just be … patient.'

He nodded and then his hands were rough on her inner thighs, prying them wide. Before he grabbed himself and slid the head of his cock along her moist entrance, he pinched her inner thigh. Just hard enough to bring everything into sharp focus. Just hard enough to make her vision sparkle with light and make her forget her impending tears.

'You seem to like a tiny hint of pain with your pleasure, did you know?' He cocked his head, grinning.

'Actually, no,' she admitted, watching him. And as if in slow motion, he pinched her again. Not too hard, not too soft – just right. And a flood of her own juices graced the top of her thighs.

Nick groaned and said, 'See, that's what I mean.'

His fingers delved into her to test her and stretch her and tease. And then he shook his head and said to her earlobe, 'Enough play. I need this. I need *you*.'

He slid into her, his big working-man hands pinning her hips to the leather seat. She was unable to move and it thrilled her through her chest and in her heart. She was entirely his – at his mercy. He fucked her slowly, watching her face like she held secrets. Casey tried to rise up to meet him, but he pushed her firmly down and moved into her as he wanted.

'Don't run from me,' he said. It wasn't the first time he'd said it.

'I won't.'

'Show me.'

So she did. She wrapped her arms around him and when he released her hips, her legs looped around his waist. Nick slipped his hands beneath her hips and tilted her just so. He drove into her deep and when he was fully in her, stretching her in the most delicious way, Casey tilted her hips up a bit more and gasped when that extra zing of pleasure coursed through her.

The first slow spasm came over her and he bit her lip lightly as she whimpered. Nick didn't pull free of her, he simply stayed sunken deep and rocked, his hips a slow motion roll from one side to the other, nudging that sweet bundle of nerve endings that had her grasping at him like a drowning woman.

'I won't run,' she promised freely as the orgasm slammed her. Her hips shot up and she bit him so that he growled.

'Don't come, don't come,' she begged and pulled herself back so he was forced to pull out.

It was comical really, the clown car effect, and they were both laughing but in a needy rushed way as they switched. When Casey had him under her, she splayed her palms on his hard chest and, even through his nice fancy shirt, she could feel his heart pounding.

She sank down on him slowly, watching the feed of his cock into her body. Watching the way he bit his lip to keep control and his hands restlessly balled into fists on the leather seat. She put her hands over his hands and forced him to be still.

'Let me,' she said and pressed her breasts to him, kissing him. 'And when we get home, I want to do this all again. Utterly naked. Not like horny teenagers.'

Nick chuckled, grabbed her wild mess of long hair and tugged her in for a kiss. His tongue stroked over hers and Casey could feel the urgency of his impending release on that kiss. 'Admit it, though. Horny teenagerdom is fun?

She rotated her hips in a slow sensuous dance, feeling the grind of his pelvic bone to her clitoris. Feeling the friction of his cock in her most sensitive places. Feeling the power of her emotions and how much she cared for him already. It was overwhelming to her and even though she was supposed to be in charge, she let his hands go when the force of her release hit and he grabbed her hips to hold her tight. Driving up under her, he watched her face and when he came he just said, 'Casey ... Casey.'

Chapter Ten

'TAKE ME HOME,' SHE whispered. 'You have to do my bidding. I'm the highest bidder.'

Nick shook his head, smiling as he drove her car through the light rain that had started. It was late afternoon and the car smelled like sex. Which turned her on.

'You were the *only* bidder,' he reminded her.

'Yeah, what was that about? That makes zero sense.'

He turned on to her street and parked in the driveway. Casey had never been so happy to be such a short distance from the Manchester Hotel.

He cut the engine and turned to her. Her panties were sticking out of her purse and cool air was drifting up under her skirt. She wanted him again. It was an almost violent need.

She grabbed him and kissed him hard, tugging his hair so a rumble sounded in his chest.

'I told you that would happen,' he said.

'Bullshit,' Casey said. She unlocked the door and kicked it wide before remembering her "bare ass naked under her skirt" status. Hopefully, none of her neighbours were watching. 'I smell a rat. A very short but adorable rat named Annie.'

'Five thousand dollars!' He laughed, almost chasing her up the walkway. Casey let out a squeal and when he managed a just-rough-enough swat on her ass, she shrieked like a lunatic.

New love …

It hit her like a fist but she kept going. She refused to let herself freak out.

'It was my five thousand dollars,' she said to him, barely managing to shove her key in the door before he pressed himself up against her and hustled her in.

'No. It was mine.'

She shook her head and dropped her purse by the door. 'Nope. Yours is in my purse. I'll be writing them a cheque. I bought you, boy.' She tugged his collar and pushed big burly Nick to the wall. Then she smashed her body to his, feeling the hardness of his chest under her breasts and the rising ridge of his cock to her pussy lips.

'There's way too much fabric between us,' he said.

'I agree.' Casey yanked his tie loose and started on the buttons.

'It'll be faster if we just–'

She kissed him fiercely, running her tongue over his plump kiss-bruised lips and broke free to ditch her skirt and her blouse and everything else in her way in an untidy heap.

Naked, they hit the sofa with a soft exhalation of air and more urgent kisses.

'Turn around.'

'What?'

'Turn. Around.' His eyes were darker blue when he was insistent.

She turned her back to him thinking he'd get up behind her. Fuck her doggie style. Instead, he pulled her so she straddled his face. His charming pink tongue darted out and she watched on hands and knees as he started to lap at her in soft, gentle strokes.

Her hair tickled her face and she sighed, not sure if she was more turned on by the heated softness of his tongue on her clit – dragging slowly so she felt the urge to lower herself more and prod him on – or the sight of him.

He was hard against her cheek and she inhaled the salted scent of their coupling on his cock. The skin, silk and steel against her face. Perfection.

Just to make him crazy, she pressed the damp tip of her tongue – held rigid and still – to the slit at the top. The ocean-flavoured drop of precome made her cave though. Along with the noise he made – half desperation, half aggression.

She sucked his cock into her mouth slowly, savouring every salty inch. Her tongue swirled and played over the ridges of veins and the smooth sheath. She managed to get him all the way in by relaxing her throat and it was then that he clamped his mouth over her pussy, applying perfect suction and the slippery nudges of his tongue pushed her over the edge.

She came with a long moan stifled by the length of him in her mouth, in her throat.

Nick thrust up under her, once, twice and she prepared herself to swallow him down the way he was swallowing her. He continued to probe and lick, extracting every sugary spasm from her orgasm. Casey, played her tongue over him and felt him driving up just a bit more – a controlled but chaotic rhythm that said he was close. So fucking close.

Her fingers tickled over his balls, her hair brushing his thighs. She bobbed her head, willing him to give it up but he whispered, 'Let me up.'

She thought about arguing, but the thought of him fucking her, penetrating her – taking her –won out and she moved for him.

Nick dragged her to the floor and pressed her breasts and belly to the sofa.

'I love your back when I fuck you like this,' he said in her ear, his tongue sliding along her throat, smothering her pulse. 'I love the way you look – like a painting.'

He gripped her hips hard and drove into her – rough without preamble.

Possessive

She almost came when the thought flitted through her head, a luminescent butterfly of a thought.

He fucked her in short thrusts that banged her belly to the cushions. His fingers reached around to find her – firm and slippery. Small brutal circles brought her closer and closer and Casey ground her clit to his whirling fingers.

Nick's voice had come down to a rasp. He nibbled her earlobe hard enough to make her nipples pebble and her cunt flex. But it was when he growled, 'Mine,' as he came that she lost it.

Casey came with him, her body splayed against the sofa, her hair tangled around her face. All she could hear was his breath and her heart and the blood banging between them as they came. And for one second she wasn't sure where he started and she ended.

And that was fine by her.

'Read this,' she said, putting her feet on the coffee table. They were freshly showered and dressed in sweats. He looked cute in her sweats. Thank God she was tall and liked to keep some XLs in the house. Or he'd look like a ballerina.

The thought made her snort.

Nick took her phone and read.

'Holy shit.'

'I told you that they'd bid on you.'

'But–'

'But my best friend, Annie, decided Cupid also had to be like a mob enforcer. She told all the women not to bid on you or else.'

'Or else what?'

Casey shrugged. 'Who knows? She's such a busybody, she probably has dirt on most of the women there. She was bluffing and they bought it.'

'Wow,' he said, laughing and shaking his head.

Casey sighed, 'She's protective of me.'

'I can imagine.' He took another sip of wine and toed her foot with his. She'd even seen fit to lend him a pair of her favourite cold weather socks. Wool men's hunting socks with a khaki green stripe at the top. Add one of her many oversized promotional charity sweatshirts and he looked lazy, laid back and lickable.

'I don't need it – the protection,' she said, pushing her shoulders back.

He just looked at her, smiling slightly.

'At least not any more. I finally have ... moved forward some, I guess.'

'I hope that means me.' He took her hand.

'It means you.' She squeezed.

'So, what's next? I'm all yours. Five thousand dollars worth.'

'Ah, I like the sound of that. I'm thinking order in Italian from the place up the street and then ...' Casey toed the crotch of his sweatpants. Her feet were sheathed in rugged cotton Fair Isle socks, they looked very festive stimulating his cock.

'And then?' Nick put his wine down and pushed her back on the sofa, kissing her neck, nibbling her clavicle so she shivered.

'And then I want to see you all nekkid again,' she snickered. 'To make sure I got my money's worth.'

Nick eyed her, suddenly serious. He touched her lips, stroked her cheekbone. 'Did you, Casey? Did you get your money's worth?'

He sounded so worried her heart broke a little. When she let herself be calm and think about it, she could imagine a business with him. Dinners with him. Reading a book silently next to him. Hikes and travelling and lots of laughter and lots of sex. She wasn't brave enough to say it all yet. Not yet, but close. She was getting there. But he needed to know something, *something* of how she felt of him.

Casey looked him in the eye as she pulled his face forward, running her thumbs over the stubble blooming on his strong jaw. 'You, Nick Murphy ... you are *priceless*.'

More great titles in
The Secret Library

Silk Stockings
9781908262042

One Long Hot Summer
9781908262066

Traded Innocence
9781908262028

The Game
9781908262103

Hungarian Rhapsody
9781908262127

Hungarian Rhapsody – Justine Elyot

Ruby had no idea what to expect from her trip to Budapest, but a strange man in her bed on her first night probably wasn't it. Once the mistake is ironed out, though, and introductions made, she finds herself strangely drawn to the handsome Hungarian, despite her vow of holiday celibacy. Does Janos have what it takes to break her resolve and discover the secrets she is hiding, or will she be able to resist his increasingly wild seduction tactics? Against the romantic backdrop of a city made for lovers, personalities clash. They also bump. And grind.

Restraint – Charlotte Stein

Marnie Lewis is certain that one of her friends – handsome but awkward Brandon – hates her guts. The last thing she wants to do is go on a luscious weekend away with him and a few other buddies, to a cabin in the woods. But when she catches Brandon doing something very dirty after a night spent listening to her relate some of her *sexcapades* to everyone, she can't resist pushing his buttons a little harder. He might seem like a prude, but Marnie suspects he likes a little dirty talk. And Marnie has no problems inciting his long dormant desires.

A Sticky Situation – Kay Jaybee

If there is a paving stone to trip over, or a drink to knock over, then Sally Briers will trip over it or spill it. Yet somehow Sally is the successful face of marketing for a major pharmaceutical company; much to the disbelief of her new boss, Cameron James.

Forced to work together on a week-long conference in an Oxford hotel, Sally is dreading spending so much time with arrogant new boy Cameron, whose presence somehow makes her even clumsier than usual.

Cameron, on the other hand, just hopes he'll be able to stay professional, and keep his irrational desire to lick up all the accidentally split food and drink that is permanently to be found down Sally's temptingly curvy body, all to himself.

218